THE BATTLES OF THRAE:

In Search of Aragopia

T. Christopher Byrd

L&Z Productions, LLC

In Search of Aragopia

Copyright © 2012

L&Z Productions, LLC

www.TheBattlesofThrae.com

Made in the United States of America

An Introduction

(A Quick History of this New World)

There was once, or maybe there will be (depending on the beginnings of such things) a great land in its early times, where many areas were still empty and the only known people still lived amongst each other, not having a long enough history to conquer all that there was in this land. A planet actually, a planet called Thrae.

Many secrets and misrepresented histories exist so that no one, except perhaps the author, knows the true beginnings and the exact history of this world, though that is limited, as there are unlimited histories yet to be imagined.

The history of Thrae that is known, mostly by the older people, begins with a god-like being. This being called himself Kron. Where this being came from and how he came upon his power is, of course for later, much later, as this is only a part of a long adventure that will go beyond the times of this era and further back, as the people of Thrae discover more and more about the history of their young planet.

After creating Thrae, Kron filled it with plants and creatures for the land, water and air to give this planet life. Kron then created a being, similar to himself. A creature that would be more advanced than any of his other creations. He called this being Alohessy and placed him on Thrae to watch over and take care of all that he had made.

Alohessy was given great powers. Many would call them magical powers, though he was not as powerful as his creator. For all the powers that Alohessy possessed, his heart and caring for others was minimal and he became more of a savage than a shepherd to this beautiful planet. Kron grew annoyed by Alohessy, so he created another like him and called him Chryson. Chryson had almost as much power as Alohessy, but Kron made sure that he cared more for the things of Thrae than did his counterpart.

Almost immediately Alohessy and Chryson began to battle. They were too close in power for either to overtake the other, and they were not able to be killed, though actions by Alohessy will change that fact later, so they began using their powers to create creatures of their own. Since these creatures were for battle and meant to kill, they were evil creatures and nothing of the sort that

Kron ever wished upon his planet.

Desiring to improve on his creations, Kron created Brigal. Brigal had less power than the other two and he had a warmer heart. Not warm enough, as, out of fear of the power of Alohessy, Brigal joined with him. This alliance turned the tide in the battles with Chryson.

Kron was annoyed by his three mistakes and he tried again. He created a being with limited powers, but with caring and love for all things so strong, that it would never join in the battles that were destroying the world he created. She was female, a less aggressive version than the male. Her name was Dorisha. Dorisha avoided the battles, but was alone and saddened, so Kron created her a son. This creation was like a human. He had no special powers, but his heart and soul were as powerful as anything ever created by Kron. Kron had figured out how to create spirit and the spirit in man will become the answer to many troubling times ahead. Dorisha named her son Doran and he grew up in hiding as the battles between Alohessy and Brigal against Chryson intensified.

Alohessy, being the most powerful, created a sword capable of killing Chryson. Of course a sword capable of killing one being is capable of killing the others like him. Alohessy eventually killed Chryson and intended on reigning over all of Thrae. He also intended on taking Dorisha as his wife, so as to have offspring, which would own powers similar to themselves.

While the battles raged on, Doran grew and Kron was so impressed by this human, he created more. He created many humans, fully grown so as to increase the population quickly. Kron knew that Alohessy would not like these humans and knew that he would be a great threat to them. Eventually Alohessy did discover the humans and began to kill any that crossed his path. These actions angered Kron and he created a race of warriors. These creatures were called Legnas, and they were created solely to fight Alohessy and Brigal and their evil creations.

Kron lead the Legnas against Alohessy and his creatures, but the Legnas were not as powerful as Alohessy and the evil of his army. Kron was so fearful of creating another Alohessy that he did not give the Legnas enough power, resulting in Kron's army being defeated and him being captured.

Kron was immortal and therefore couldn't be killed, so as part of Alohessy's plan, he was tricked into going into the Caves of Talpri. Below the Pryon Mountains which lie in the northern lands, was a labyrinth of mines that were so complicated that even Kron, once deep enough, could not find his way out.

Realizing that the humans posed a threat, Alohessy decided he needed offspring and kidnapped Dorisha. He told Kron that she was in the Caves of Talpri and Kron went to look for her and in his desperate search, lost his way and was imprisoned.

Alohessy left Brigal in charge of the battles with the humans and he took Dorisha to his lair, somewhere in the Pryon Mountains, so that he may have children.

Alohessy and Dorisha had five offspring, which were called Zircas. They had the potential to have powers similar to Alohessy's, but not as potent. They also had caring and love in their hearts, similar to Dorisha, but no matter how warm a heart starts, experiences and influences can turn it cold.

Brigal began losing to the humans. When he heard a rumor that Alohessy was coming back he became very scared. He knew the wrath of Alohessy and knew his losses against the humans would not be taken lightly. He abandoned the war and went into hiding.

Alohessy returned to see that his creations had almost become extinct. Angered, Alohessy killed Dorisha and set out to destroy all the humans himself. Having the advantage of being immortal, he knew it would take a long time, but eventually he would conquer, what he considered annoying pests.

In Alohessy's rage, he made a critical error. The humans were very intelligent and were very good at strategy. Alohessy was drawn away from the cave where he kept his five Zirca. A human named Ranishi, a young and very talented warrior had stolen Alohessy's sword and he assassinated the evil being with it.

Ranishi became a hero and a central character in many tales. Whether true, false or exaggerated, may one day be known, but soon after leading the humans to victory over Alohessy's evil minions, Ranishi disappeared. Many believed he went to the Utopian land of Aragopia, rumors of which had been brought to the attention of humans, which was supposedly created by Brigal to make up for all his sins. They were only rumors, though.

Some believed Ranishi may have been killed by an evil Fikron, a large black cat-like creature created by Alohessy. Some even said that Ranishi had set out to find Kron, to release him from his prison under the Pryon Mountains. Perhaps one day, the truth will be known.

Now began the rule of man on Thrae. The five Zirca were separated amongst the people, now making up four tribes. The main two tribes were the Trett and the Arizz. The other two were smaller, the Suna-Noru and the Miklidor. The Zircas were never told of their bloodline and they lived as humans, not knowing any difference. Even younger generations were not told of the origins of the Zirca, though it became hard at times to explain the Zirca's extremely long lifespan.

See, Zirca have the ability to have many great powers, but they must learn them. The humans intended on never revealing these truths to the five Zirca, and that was the plan. Of course nothing ever goes as planned.

Many generations went by. There were battles between humans, there was the evil orphan Tiriach, who took over the tribe called Miklidor and searched out the Zircas to teach them their history and their magic, in order to attempt to take over all the lands. A war broke out, but eventually the humans defeated the Zircas, led by two brothers, Plythagor and Jeroquy. The tribes joined as one and peace was over the land.

Of course, humans are flawed and they disagree. So much so that they become violent against each other and even brothers may fight, and so did Plythagor and Jeroquy, and half the people followed Jeroquy and half followed Plythagor and once again the people were split into two warring tribes, the Trett and the Arizz. Plythagor was assassinated and Jeroquy disappeared, but the battles continued.

The Arizz held the Great City, and if you held the city, you were the holders of the kingdom. The Trett lived in colonies, on the borders of the outlands. They were led by a bloodthirsty man called The General. The General held a deep hate for the Arizz and was determined to conquer and take the city. The Arizz were losing the war and due to a weak king who made bad decisions, The General was closer and closer to winning this conflict.

The Arizz leadership decided, against the protests of many, including those of a peace activist politician named Salazaar, to create a military academy for all male youth, starting at age six and to be ready for battle at age 16.

So begins our journey.

Chapter 1

The Great City stands in the middle of a vast prairie. In the distance, rolling hills fill the horizon, like a brown sea in rough weather. The city is surrounded on all sides by massive walls that are built high enough that it would require the tallest ladders in all the land for an enemy to ever breach them and conquer the city. The only way in is through two huge, heavy duty gates on the east side of the city. Though they are left open on normal days, the massive doors can quickly swing shut at the threat of attack.

The city is littered with many buildings, houses, and markets. People feel safe inside the walls and walk freely to and fro, shopping at the markets, sitting in the courtyard, eating, talking and some performing. Many guards stand atop the walls watching for any incoming armies, which in these times is more and more often. It is a great city, and a great prize for the conqueror of this land.

In a far corner of the city stands the youth military academy. Several buildings cover the grounds and are where most of the classrooms are located. This is where the youth receive basic education and learn military tactics. The classes are taught by the mentors, experienced warriors, with some being heroes of past wars, but now too old for battle. Each mentor is assigned two or three boys, to teach them the ways and guide them to becoming great warriors.

Outside of the school building is a large open area, set up to simulate a battlefield. There are varying terrains and makeshift buildings and bunkers. Mock battles constantly take place. When a boy isn't in the classroom, he is taking part in a battle drill. The boys spend most of their time at the academy, but they live at home with their parents or guardians like normal kids.

This story follows five of those boys.

It is break time on a cloudless, sunny day at the academy. The blue sky is so peaceful it could easily make you forget that this was a time of war. With the light, cool breeze blowing across the prairie, cooling the face on a warm day, one would be apt to take a carefree nap as to be cautious of the ever present threat of invasion.

Zerin stands on the academy grounds watching a mock battle taking place on the field. The boys all wear similar clothing. They wear a long green hooded robe with no sleeves over a brown longsleeve undershirt. They have loose brown pants which are covered by high leather boots, bound by leather straps. The outfit is good for all situations, from bad weather to battle and is the preferred wear of Arizz youth.

Zerin, a twelve year old standout at the academy has long brown hair and is built like a typical kid of his age. He has an innocence in his appearance that hides the skills that he possesses for the art of war. His hazel eyes often express his deep thinking personality and a quiet stress shows in his expressions as his mind analyzes all situations. Today as he studies the other students, he analyzes their demeanors to determine who is brave and who has fear. One of his friends, named Quynn approaches. He stands next to Zerin and observes the battle as well.

Quynn is fourteen and also a standout at the academy. He is average height and very skinny, but strong. He wears his orange hair pulled back and tied. His hair is more like the adult style, revealing his age advantage over his friends. Sometimes considered impatient, he has the respect of the boys at the academy. He shows great leadership skills and is being considered for a high position in the Arizz army once he reaches sixteen.

"Where is Juntor?" asks Quynn. "You know he is always following you around."

"I'm sure he'll be around sometime. I think he had to stay late in a class for something."

"Probably been slacking off on his school work," says Quynn, also known for his limited sympathy.

"Well, he has troubles at home, so he has a lot to deal with," answers Zerin.

One stand out quality of Zerin is his merciful ways. Some may call it conflicted, though others may say he learns from two sides of the argument when it comes to war. While

Zerin trains daily at the military academy learning all things war, his home life is much different. His father, Salazaar, is a politician and very much against war, so when Zerin gets home every day, he hears arguments for peace. A smart young man at only twelve, Zerin takes the pros and cons from both sides and tries to find the right decision for every problem.

"There he is," says Quynn pointing toward Juntor.

"Try to be nice to him. He doesn't take criticism too well and he is only ten," says Zerin.

Juntor approaches. He is a smaller and younger than the other two and is a little chubby which opens him up to more ridicule from those who would say he is lazy. He walks with a sluggish gait, which many see as another sign of laziness. The truth is that he carries the weight of an abusive home life on his shoulders. His father is a drunk and his mother left him when he was little. He tries to keep his home secrets at home, but many of the elders know of the abuse, including Salazaar. This is how Zerin knows and why he tries to be a friend to Juntor. Juntor is fond of Zerin as well and depends on Zerin to get him through some of the harder days.

"Hey guys," says Juntor.

The boys nod at Juntor and they all continue watching the battle drill. Senokre walks over with Lach.

"Gentleman," greets Senokre.

Senokre is eleven years old, tall for his age and has very tan skin. He wears his brown hair shorter than most. The girls in the city all have crushes on him, but he "has little time for the weaker sex, we have a war to win," as he would often say, boldly. Senokre is also a top prospect for the Arizz army, once he comes of age.

Quynn looks at Lach and in an effort to tease him says, "Wow, those are some really tough guys on the field. I guess we would have our hands full against them."

Lach glares at the boys on the field for a few moments. Of the five boys he is the one that the leadership has the most hope in and the most fear. Lach is an orphan and lives with his mentor, Olkar. Many have concluded that not having a family is the reason for his quick temper. Often having to be calmed by his friends to prevent one of his "outbreaks of rage", as some have defined it.

It isn't really rage as much as it is the fact that Lach is ready to fight at a moment's notice with only an inkling of a challenge.

He has blonde hair that is about shoulder length. Like Zerin he has micro-expressions that demonstrate a lot more going on inside his head than what can be seen. But his is not of finding the right solutions for all situations. It is more of a war-like mentality, eager to prove his power and eager to conquer anything that wrongs him.

There was one time, when an Arizz warrior snapped at a younger academy youth out in the courtyard, and though the warrior was much older and very much larger than Lach, Lach challenged and attacked the warrior. He even taunted the warrior as they battled. The warrior got the better of Lach, though he fought beyond his years. Impressed by Lach, the warrior gave him a medallion that only men of war would have. Now most Arizz youth would take great pride in the rare gift and cherish it for their life. But when Lach has a grudge, he keeps a grudge and spat upon the medallion, rubbed it in the dirt and threw it back at the warrior.

Lach looks at the boys on the field and smirks. "They don't look like much to me."

Quynn smiles at Zerin who then sees Lach look at him and roll his eyes. Zerin smiles, then looks to Senokre.

"Can't you keep him in line, Senokre?"

"I gave up on making any attempt to control him. He is like a Fikron in human form."

Quynn laughs, "Fikron! Been visiting that crazy old man again? If you make company of fools, it will eventually rub off on you."

Senokre responds, "That crazy old man has been around for a long time, and has seen a lot of things that many of the elders will not share with us youth. I believe his stories about the Fikron."

"I do not," counters Quynn.

"As a matter of fact," says Senokre, "I am going to speak with him this afternoon. I have read about a secret land, long since forgotten. I am going to see if he has ever heard of it."

"Then what?" challenges Lach.

Senokre looks around at the boys faces. "Maybe I'll go in search of it."

Quynn, Zerin and Lach laugh. Juntor follows suit.

"You'll be eaten by a Fikron before you get there," Quynn replies, causing the rest of the boys to crack up further.

Senokre nods, accepting the ridicule but still determined to learn more about this secret land.

A bell rings to signal the end of the break. The boys set to go back to class.

"I am going right after school, if you want to go. Meet

me here and we'll all go together," Senokre says with a confidence in his voice, indicating he knows their mockery will be overtaken by their curiosity.

The boys mutter doubtful excuses as they walk in different directions to their classes.

The sun has worked its way across the sky, hovering over the horizon, as if looking for a good place to rest for the night. A bell rings, signaling what the sun has already shown, it is late afternoon. Late afternoon and the end to another school day.

Many youth exit the academy, walking to their homes or wherever they are to be on this particular afternoon. Senokre arrives at the meeting spot to find no one there. He smiles and walks to a tree a short distance away. He stands behind the tree so he will be invisible to anyone approaching from the school.

"We'll see who's too busy for a good story", he says to himself.

Zerin arrives first and looks around to see if any of the other boys are coming. He doesn't see Senokre hiding behind the tree. As is usually the case, Juntor is not far behind and stands beside his idol. Senokre decides to show himself. The two boys see him and smile.

"I knew you couldn't resist a good story," Senokre says while he looks around. "I guess Lach and Quynn aren't coming. Oh well, their loss. Are you ready to go?"

Juntor looks at Zerin for his choice.

"I'm in," responds Zerin.

Juntor peps up. "Me too!"

Senokre looks at Juntor, with a smile. "What a

surprise. Let's go."

Senokre leads the way. As the boys walk, they hear the sound of feet running up behind them. They turn to see the source of the noise. It is Lach and Quynn. Senokre smiles.

Quynn smiles and says, "Don't get excited, we just know we have to make sure the old man doesn't tell you some craziness that will make your minds turn to mush. I hear old men like that can cast spells on young boys."

Juntor looks at Quynn, wondering if his words are true.

Senokre shakes his head and turns to continue the walk. The rest of the boys follow.

The old man that the boys seek, lives in a shanty house on the outskirts of the housing area in the Great City. Juntor is intimidated by the decrepit little house as the boys arrive. It is only big enough for one room and built almost at an angle, looking as if it was the first attempt of a carpenter, if indeed a carpenter had built it at all. The front door, which doesn't exactly fit into the doorway, taunts the boys. They walk to the door. Juntor is timid and Quynn immediately notices his sudden hesitation.

"Calm down Juntor, there are no such men that can cast spells," he says to calm the scared boy, but reversing his attempts in the very next sentence, "but of course, if Senokre is right, there are many things that we do not know about."

Juntor stops in his tracks. Zerin looks at the unnerved boy.

"He is joking, Juntor. There is nothing to fear."

"I think I forgot," Juntor stumbles, searching for an excuse to get out of this mess he is no longer interested in pursuing, "uh, that my father wanted me home early to, um, do chores."

"I'm messing with you Juntor. Do not be afraid. This man knows no magic," says Quynn.

"I have to go, though," Juntor says as he hurries away.

Quynn looks at Senokre with expectation. "So knock on the door."

Senokre pauses and licks his lips, now unsure himself. He had felt different after talking with the old man a few times. Perhaps he was putting spells on him. Just as Senokre is about to speak, a voice calls from inside.

"Are you coming in, or shall I call the guard to run off the vagrants lingering in front of my house?" the voice threatens.

All the boys look around at each other.

"That's Hedgeparth. He is waiting for us," Senokre says, recognizing he is about to lose his team.

The boys hesitantly enter the shanty house. Once inside, the boys look around at the mess that includes a dirty kitchen, a table, and one chair. The house is musky and dingy. Quynn turns up his nose as he looks around.

Hedgeparth sits in the corner, on the floor, as if he was meditating or chanting some evil curse until he was interrupted by the visitors.

"Good afternoon, Hedgeparth," Senokre greets the creepy old man, "these are my friends. We have come to hear some more secret stories of the history of Thrae."

"Well, welcome. I have no food. I have only one chair and my house is a little unkempt," apologizes Hedgeparth, a small man in stature who has a big beard and bushy hair which nearly hides his face. His clothes are ragged and he smells like he has missed a few baths. His smell is pungent, even for an era like this one, where cleanliness is not a top priority. He smokes a pipe, probably depending on the smoke to hide the full offense of the odor in his house.

"Sit, sit," he demands.

The boys look for a free place to sit and reluctantly settle on the bare and very dirty floor.

Lach leans over to Quynn and whispers, "Forget spells. I believe we may have diseases after this visit."

Senokre pipes up after overhearing Lach's comment. "I have heard of a place on the outskirts of our lands. It is not on any maps that I have looked over and though I have been told some things, by various people regarding this place, they refuse to go into further detail. I have heard it is a utopian type of land, where there is magic and wonders and many things, a place where most of our people have never heard of. Do you know of any place like this?"

The old man nods his head. His eyes show his mind going back to a memory of such a place. It is hard to read if his eyes reflect pain or longing, but Senokre realizes Hedgeparth may know of what he asks.

"Oh, yes. I believe you ask about a place called Aragopia," responds Hedgeparth.

"Yes, I believe I heard that name for it from someone," Senokre says. "What can you tell us about it?"

"I have never been there, but I know of someone who has been in search of it. It is a land far to the northwest of here. It is said that Brigal created this land after..." Hedgeparth pauses, "Do you know who Brigal is?"

All the boys shake their heads, no.

Hedgeparth tells the boys a quick account of Brigal's

creation to his disappearance. Since this history is not exact, Hedgeparth tells the best of what he knows. Once the boys are up to date on who Brigal is, he continues.

"Feeling remorse for his actions, Brigal created a utopian society, where any man that lived there would no longer age, but live forever. There are supposed to be many spells, or perhaps just medicines, that can heal all our sicknesses. All of the doctors' studies and questions can be answered by one trip to Aragopia."

Zerin speaks up. "Why does everyone keep it secret, if it contains such vital information?"

"There are many reasons, but the main one, and the only one I am going to share with you, is the journey. Many evil lands lie between here and Aragopia. Evil mountains, evil caves, evil fountains, and many, many evil creatures. So dangerous that even the bravest warriors dare not take the journey. And the ones who have dared have never returned."

"How then would you know of such a place?" challenges Quynn.

"Perhaps one has attempted, but forced to turn back, before the danger took him," responds Hedgeparth.

The boys stare at Hedgeparth now, with great interest, and wait for the forthcoming story.

"I was a young man of about 20 years. I was a very curious person and found great interest in the unknown histories of our civilization."

Hedgeparth pauses to look around at the boys, who sit content, awaiting an amazing story as Senokre had promised.

Hedgeparth continues. "Because of many battles, the histories of this land are jumbled up, mixed up, changed to benefit the conquering tribe, or destroyed due to accident or design and therefore it is hard to connect the dots. But, I did learn that I am a descendant of the Suna-Noru tribe.

The Suna-Noru was a religious tribe which was eventually destroyed by an evil man called Tiriach."

Hedgeparth pauses again and thinks to himself for a moment then continues. "So I found this history and pursued further. I learned of the Pryon Mountains and the Fountains of Talpri and the Caves of Talpri. I learned of the most evil creature, which is one of the few that still exist from Alohessy's reign."

"The Fikron?" Senokre interjects, excited to remind some of his company who had ridiculed him earlier.

Hedgeparth's eyes widen in surprise. "You have heard of a Fikron?"

Senokre smiles and nods his head then nudges Zerin who sits beside him.

Hedgeparth continues. "Oh what evil a Fikron is. A large black cat-like creature with teeth as long as a man's finger and claws as sharp as the sharpest sword created by a master sword smith. So black, that on a night in a full moon, it could stand right beside you and you would never know it was there, until the pain of those razor sharp claws rip through your flesh and then, of course, it is too late."

Doubtful, Quynn tries to listen without care, though the hairs standing on the back of his neck are hard to ignore. Senokre's pride in his knowledge blinds him to his own growing anxiety. Zerin weighs the pros and cons as the story grows and Lach sits, no longer critical, but desiring to encounter such a great and dangerous enemy as a Fikron. As far as Juntor, it is a good thing he chose to leave, or he may have never ended up on the adventure to come.

"I could tell you more about the Fikron, as you seem very amazed by my description, or I can continue on with the story you requested to hear. It is up to you," says Hedgeparth

No words are spoken from the boys.

"Very well," starts Hedgeparth, "then I shall continue on about my adventure and the Fikron can come in later, as it is actually the cause to the end of my adventure.

After I learned all that I could about the histories of this world and trust me, they were few and far between, I planned my adventure. My goal was to find, at the end, Aragopia.

I set out alone. My plan was to go through the lands west of here that were of my ancestors, the Suna-Noru. Then I would continue going west into Miklidor, turn north and head toward the Pryon Mountains and the Caves of Talpri. These areas I had bits and pieces of maps and histories so that I had partly an idea of where I was heading, but what lay on the Pryon Mountains and in the Caves of Talpri, I only had rumor and legend to go by. And what lay past that was myth, so I was going on blind faith."

"You went by yourself?" asks Quynn.

"Yes." Answers Hedgeparth, "No one would go on such a ridiculous journey as to risk life and limb to find a place no one believed existed. Even the old timers, who knew of the histories now kept secret, had never heard of it, even after a few drinks, which by the way, is a good strategy for getting secret histories un-secreted."

Hedgeparth laughs as he has a memory of a drunken old timer who passed out in the middle of a good story.

"Please, continue with the story," says Quynn, now totally open to the possibility of Senokre's stories being true.

Hedgeparth continues. "Yes, so I made my way into Suna-Noru and found the ruins of a temple, as the Suna-Noru were a religious people, many temples were built in that land and many destroyed during the last years of the tribe as well. But anyway, I journeyed through Suna-Noru and on the border with Miklidor.

I looked forward to my journey into Miklidor, but I found my way was blocked. During the wars between the Miklidor and Suna-Noru, in order to avoid surprise, the Miklidor poisoned the lands on the border leaving only secret paths that could be safely crossed. Of course I did not know where the secret paths were and I didn't see need to test my strength against unknown poisons, so I headed north, along the line of the border. I assumed I could find a way to the Pryon Mountains without having to go through Miklidor.

An evil place is that Miklidor, though. In some areas, where I could see across, I saw bizarre mutated creatures. All were similar to the creatures we have in these lands, but perhaps due to poisons or just evil, they were deformed and grotesque and looked as if in pain with every movement they made. I hurried along, for I did not know how far into where I was that the poison reached and I did not want to give anymore access to my body than necessary.

I reached the northern border of Suna-Noru and could see in the great distance, what I believed to be the Pryon Mountains. So, I journeyed on."

Hedgeparth looks around at the boys in an attempt to read their minds. Hedgeparth loved telling stories of his old adventures and loved even more when an audience sat in stunned silence, eager for more. He continues.

"At the northern side of Suna-Noru, on the border of

Miklidor, there are scattered bunches of trees. It is very beautiful land and to see it, one may wonder why there is no tribe settled there. The trees are nice and tall, and spread far enough between each to allow the sunlight in and allow for a good spot for a camp. As you walk out from one bunch of trees you see the Pryon Mountains extending up toward the sky, with the tallest peaks white with snow. The land was so beautiful, that I thought for a moment that perhaps the maps were wrong and that Aragopia was actually on the south side of the Pryon Mountains, instead of on the north side. Either way, I decided at that moment that I would, after my journey was over, come back to this area and build a nice cabin and spend the rest of my days there, perhaps starting a family and maybe restarting the Suna-Noru."

Hedgeparth looks around at the boys with a fierce look in his eyes.

"Do not make plans like that, until you know everything there is to know about an area. I, of course, never got the chance to put my plan into action, as I soon discovered why there was no tribe or people living on the northern border of Suna-Noru and Miklidor. I journeyed far enough toward the Pryon Mountains to where I could see, with my scope what appeared to be the Fountains of Talpri.

I have heard many stories of the Fountains of Talpri, all being too farfetched even for an adventurer like me to believe, but it was a beautiful sight. I thought I should visit there, just to take a swim.

I never made it. The easiest way to the fountains that I found took me to the edge of the Caves of Talpri which bordered the fountains. I made it to the very edge of the outermost fountain, and there my journey turned dangerous.

At the edge of that very fountain, a creature crouched, having a drink. Lucky for me, I saw it before it saw me, which gave me a head start. And, though I had never seen one, not even a picture, I knew immediately what the dangerous creature was."

"A Fikron?" asks Lach, now even more interested in the story, as the existence of the Fikron seems to be coming true.

"Yes, it was a Fikron," answers Hedgeparth. "I managed to hide behind a tree before it saw me, though I believe it caught a glimpse, because it looked up from its drink and scanned the area where I was just standing. It looked around for a moment and then walked away."

"So you retreated and abandoned your journey?" asks Lach.

"I wouldn't call it a retreat, since I was not at war, but to look upon a creature like that would make even the bravest warrior have second thoughts." Hedgeparth answers, trying not to be offended.

"I will not be afraid, if we come across one of these creatures," states Lach boldly, and he was being true. While many would look to make a statement for appearance purposes, but never truly be brave enough to actually stand by their words, Lach meant what he said and when he set his mind on something, he intended on going through with it.

"Well, I do not think a Fikron would ever come into these parts. Too many men exist for it to survive," Hedgeparth points out.

Lach and Senokre look at each other. Hedgeparth picks up on the look and figures out what the boys are considering.

"You do not intend on going anywhere near those areas, do you?" asks Hedgeparth. "I would not recommend anyone, without an army; ever go to those places, especially a small group of boys."

Lach frowns at Hedgeparth and speaks his mind, especially when he feels his abilities are put in question. "I believe anyone who cowers at the first sign of trouble and turns away from his mission has no say in who is or is not able to go on such journeys."

Zerin puts his hand on Lach's shoulder. Though he was virtually impossible to calm down once he was set on his warpath, Lach trusted Zerin and calms a bit when his best friend attempts to ease his intensity.

Lach looks at Zerin and says, "Does he not know that we are trained warriors? Trained specifically to save the kingdom from the evil Trett?"

"I know very well of your training. I do not underestimate what you are training, but you are still in training and therefore not ready for such a journey, and much less able to call yourself a warrior," answers Hedgeparth.

"Again you have insulted us, old man," responds Lach.

Senokre steps in. "Everybody calm down. Hedgeparth speaks out of caring for our wellbeing, not to insult us. I understand what you say, Hedgeparth, but to go or not go on this journey will be ours as a group to decide."

"I do not pretend to have the power to tell you what you can't do. I just don't think it safe for a group of boys to go on a journey that could end their lives. Perhaps wait till you are grown."

Lach shakes his head. "I do not take advice from a man who cowers at the first sign of trouble. To go on a mission to discover something you have a passion for and to abandon it, that is cowardly."

Lach stands and looks around at his friends and says, "I will leave now, before I am insulted any further or before I hear about running from a creature that, for all I know, could be of the size and threat of an old lady's pet cat."

Lach walks to the door. Hedgeparth stands and holds the bottom of his shirt and speaks. "I never said I abandoned my trip when I saw the Fikron." Hedgeparth pulls up his shirt revealing his chest and stomach which is mangled with gruesome scars. His right side looks as if half of his rib cage had been ripped out and the scars of what appear to be slashes, like a carcass after claws had been tearing into it, and after the jaws of a predator had taken a bite.

The boys stare in horror. Quynn looks away. Zerin and Senokre study his mangled torso with shock. Lach's anger toward the old man changes to anger against a creature that would do this to a member of the Arizz tribe, as he is fiercely loyal and protective of his people.

"How did you escape?" asks Senokre.

"I was half to death and my vision blurred, but I believe I saw a man approach and the Fikron ran off. The man disappeared and I crawled with all my might as far as I could. Luckily for me I was found by some outlanders and they took me in until I was able to return here. I am no coward and for that I have spent most of my life crippled and deformed."

Lach looks at Hedgeparth before he exits and says, "I apologize for calling you a coward, but there is no amount of fear that will keep me from going on this journey. And if I do come across one of these Fikrons, I will test its skills and show it mine."

Lach leaves the house. Zerin and Quynn get up and nod goodbye to Hedgeparth and follow Lach out the door. Senokre shakes the old man's hand.

"I do not pretend to tell you what to do, but I do recommend putting off till later, this adventure that you seek," says Hedgeparth.

"I will consider your suggestion, though I fear Lach may be set on a mission now, and I have never seen him turn from his intentions," responds Senokre.

"Be careful with that Lach. His anger controls his decisions and if you do decide to go on this adventure, someone like that will look for trouble where there is already enough trouble waiting," Hedgeparth states then leans in to Senokre and whispers something in his ear. Senokre nods his head and then exits the house, joining his friends waiting outside.

None of the boys speak as they walk home. Many questions occupy their minds about the story of the old man. The only words spoken are the "goodbyes" or "see you laters" as they go their separate ways toward their homes for the evening.

Chapter 2

A cloudy day blocks the sun, giving a sense of uncertainty about the coming weather. Like the boys approaching decision, it is unknown which direction the mood will take.

Lach and Zerin walk and discuss the adventure.

"What do you think about going to find that place?" Lach asks.

"I don't know. It seems very dangerous. I am curious to go on this adventure, but I do not think I would like to face a Fikron, or any other bizarre dangerous creature that may be along the way," Zerin answers.

"I want to go, but I believe it wise for more than one to go. I do not fear the Fikron, but I do not want to be caught off guard," says Lach.

"Though, I will go alone if I have to, but I hope there will be some that are brave enough and loyal enough to go along with me." Lach says this as he gives a look to Zerin, which Zerin knows all too well. A look that basically demands that he join him, if he is the friend that he says he is.

Zerin sighs and answers, "If you choose to go on this journey, I will go with you."

Running footsteps come up behind the two boys. It is Senokre. His face shows that he has some important information.

"Quynn's father was injured in battle. He may not live," he says to the boys.

"What happened?" asks Zerin.

"What I have heard was that he was ambushed by some Trett warriors. He fought them off though his unit was outnumbered and he was badly injured, but he managed to escape," answers Senokre.

"Should we go see him?" asks a concerned Zerin.

"I do not believe they are allowing anyone in, except family."

Lach stands silently listening. As is common of Lach, he is angered by the events and searching for a way to get revenge against the Trett. Of course being only twelve years old, it is not going to happen, at least not now. Even Lach, in all his militant ways, knows that he is too young to take on an entire army. But he doesn't forget and he most definitely doesn't forgive, so he tucks it away in an already angry mind, for later, so that one day his wrath may be felt by all his enemies. And though it has nothing to do with this adventure, this wrath will play a part in major events in the not too distant future, but for now it gets tucked away.

So realizing that there is nothing they can do about Quynn's situation, the boys go about their business. They do, though, decide to meet later at their secret meeting place.

Lach goes home and since he lives with his mentor from the military academy, he learns more military tactics and fighting strategies. As angry as Lach seems at times, he is amazingly content with his home life. Lach's only real frustration in life is the years he has to wait before he becomes an adult. Because surely when he is an adult, he can avenge all the things he feels driven to avenge, or at least this is how he, as child, perceives adulthood. Of course if you are a child, you will not understand, but if you are now an adult, you know that nothing is exactly as you fantasized as a youth.

Zerin goes home to his peace activist, politician father, Salazaar. Salazaar of course, is bent on opposing anything military. Though Zerin is taken care of and has everything a boy his age could need, his home life is not a happy one. Zerin doesn't seem to have the bonds with his parents as most children usually have with their own. So from the outside, Zerin seems to have it all, but to be inside Zerin's mind, there is conflict and confusion and though he has very mature patience, he has as much tucked away in him as Lach.

Perhaps one day his patience will end, and his wrath will play a major part in events of the future, but that's for other stories.

Senokre's home life is normal and there is nothing much to be said about it, other than the fact that it is such a basic and normal life, that it increases the drive in him to look for excitement. Obviously this adventure, if he can get his friends to go along, will bring much excitement, maybe even more than a bored youth would have wished for.

So the boys spend time at their homes, going about business as usual, making sure not to reveal their secret plans for this evening. The plan, of course, is to wait till it is really late and all their family members are in bed or getting ready for bed. This was the best time for each boy, who had their own way of sneaking out of their houses, to get away undetected. It had worked many times before and it would work this time.

It is a dark night. The stars in the sky are very clear, most of the clouds from the day have moved on. The moon looks like crescent, resembling some dangerous fighting weapon, as if it has grown tired of the dominance of the sun, and lays in wait to ambush its opposite and claim the glory of the sky.

There is little activity in the Great City at this hour and a few fire lit lights still twinkle in a few buildings. The night time guards stand on top of the city walls, struggling to stay awake and continue their duty of watching for any approaching enemy. The conditions make for good cover for young boys to sneak through the city relatively undetected.

The secret meeting spot is not as much a secret place as it is a secret that the boys would sneak there late at night for meetings. Located in a small area on a far corner of the training field of the military academy, it was usually a lookout point used during mock battles. It served as a lookout point for the meetings as well. It is a small building with windows on all four sides. Inside there are benches for sitting. It has no roof, so at night you can see the stars. Often Juntor would sleep there when his father was in an abusive mood.

This of course is how Juntor, who was scared away from any idea of such adventure, comes to be involved. This particular night, Juntor's father was in a foul mood and Juntor had worked his way to the lookout point and had just gotten comfortable to begin to fade away into sleep and dreams when he is awakened by voices coming toward the little building. He looks out one of the windows, but cannot make out who the three images are. The darkness hides their identities but he does recognize the voices. They are Senokre, Lach, and Zerin.

Though Zerin knew of Juntor's abusive father, Juntor believed the others did not and Juntor was embarrassed for them to know. Being the youngest, he felt he had the most to prove, and to him, for these older guys to know that his father beat him, would show how weak he was. Though it was obvious that his father's abuse in no way meant that he was weak and in no way meant that something was wrong with him, he was only ten and didn't know enough about life to realize that none of that which his father did, was his fault.

So he keeps it secret where he can and he hides from the boys, but keeps close enough to overhear what they are meeting about.

Senokre arrives first, followed by Zerin. Lach enters with a distressed look on his face. They all sit down and turn their attention toward Lach.

Lach speaks. "I went with Olkar earlier to see how Quynn's father was doing. I saw Quynn and spoke with him. I told him about the meeting and that we would most likely go on the journey. He said he would like to go, but felt he must stay by his father's side. His hopes are high that his father will live, so I do not think he will be coming with us."

"Is that why you carry such a stressed look on your face?" asks Zerin.

Lach sighs and answers, "I asked Olkar how Quynn's father was doing and he did not have the same hope that Quynn had. He didn't know if he would even live through the night."

Senokre shakes his head. "I do not know what I would do without my father."

The boys take a moment to absorb the news about their friend then get on with the business at hand. They discuss their plans, as they have decided that they would definitely go on this adventure. They discuss routes and how to avoid running into any Trett warriors. They discuss supplies and things necessary to survive for a journey like this. Occasionally they disagree, but all in all they come to consensus on the plan.

Juntor remains outside of the little hut, hearing all the plans. Of course earlier, Juntor was scared away before he heard the stories of the old man, but that fear will not play a part in his decision to join the journey, because he is not aware of what awaits them all on this journey and all that is on his mind is to follow Zerin, as usual, wherever he goes.

He knows though, that they will not allow him on the journey. But he has plans of his own. He is going to secretly follow them just out of site as far as he can, until they are too far from the city to turn back and he will reveal himself.

The morning that marks the beginning of their great adventure is perfect for starting out on such a mission. The sun has almost exposed its entire rounded form, clearly surviving any attempts by the moon to stop its rise. The sky is blue and a small breeze blows a few clouds across the sky, like white ships sailing on a great ocean adventure on calm seas. A very nice day, almost enough to make young adventurers remember they are only boys and a day of play and games might be more tempting.

Of course these boys are different, and even if any of them ever did have such temptations, Lach would squash any alternative options.

Senokre, Lach and Zerin meet just outside of the city walls at a small wooded area surrounded by the open prairie. Each checks his supplies and readies for the journey ahead. They carry with them, a backpack with all the essentials. They have their swords bound to their sides, which is the way they always carry their weapon. They look toward the distance and take deep breaths.

Just west of the wooded area is an area of large boulders. There Juntor spies on the boys, backpack in hand, awaiting their next move.

"If we are ready and double checked, I say we get going," says Zerin.

Senokre nods. "I am ready."

"As am I," chimes in Lach.

"We shall head straight north, till we get to the outland borders. We should avoid any Trett if we take that route. We should reach there by night and we can camp," Senokre says to remind everyone.

Senokre leads the way, followed by Zerin and then Lach. Juntor watches until the boys are a good distance away and as he is about to leave the secrecy of the boulders, in the corner of his eye, he notices movement and quickly slips back behind a large boulder. He peeks around to see what caught his eye.

Running away from the Great City is a boy who is calling for the other boys to wait. It is Quynn. He runs to the wooded area and past, as Juntor watches cautiously. Juntor sees Lach notice Quynn first and tell the other boys to wait. Quynn joins the crew and they continue on. Juntor glances once more toward the Great City, just to make sure there will be no more surprise guests on this mission. When he feels it is safe, he exits and hurriedly yet cautiously follows.

The first part of the journey takes the boys over the prairie lands which surround the Great City. The land is full of rolling hills. Easy would it would be to ambush an enemy in this terrain. Lach thinks of these things as his mind, is rarely not, on war.

Zerin looks upon the land differently. He sees the beauty in it and thinks of what a waste of such peace and beauty to the horrors of war.

Senokre is indifferent to the terrain as his mind is set on the goal of the mission, finding Aragopia. Similar is Quynn, though there is more on his mind than he reveals.

The boys did not expect anything unusual on this part of their journey, but little did they know of the many battles on these prairies. As they cross over one of the high hills of the rolling land, they see in the distance to the west, what appears to be an old abandoned structure.

"Is that a fort?" asks Zerin.

"I do not know, but let us go and see," answers Lach.

So the boys turn west and head for the fort. It is about a mile from where they stopped. Excitement of their first discovery pushes them as they run, as easily excitable young men do. Over a few hills and down through a few low areas and the boys stop a short distance from the fort.

"It looked abandoned from back there, but we should be careful. There is always the threat of the Trett even if we are outside of the battle zones," says Quynn.

The boys peek over the last hill and observe the fort. It is clearly abandoned and run down. The fort is surrounded by walls, where in many places are torn down. The gate to the fort sits hanging by one hinge, obviously torn open during some siege of a past battle. The boys, after a moment of observing and feeling safe enough, approach the ruin.

They stop at the broken gate and look around at each other, each waiting for someone to lead the way in.

Lach speaks up, looking at Senokre, "what do you wait for, Senokre? You are the leader of this journey. Enter."

"What if some sort of foul creature has decided to make its home here? What if several live here, just waiting for a meal?" says a concerned Senokre.

"Then we shall draw our sword and be on guard. Forget not that we are warriors of the Arizz. There is no creature, or creatures that can stand our wrath. Let us enter, and dare any living thing to test our skills," Lach says, drawing his sword.

The boys draw their swords and enter the old fort, with Lach in the lead. It is small with a few buildings. The boys look around. There are some bones spread about and they are not sure, as well as not interested in knowing if they are human bones. There are a few broken swords and broken helmets spread about. Clearly this is a place that had been overrun by an enemy.

"Who would this fort have belonged to, the Arizz or

the Trett?" asks Zerin.

"I do not see any markings that are familiar to me," says Lach.

The boys walk along the edge of the wall. The fort is small enough for them to see everything that is inside from one spot, though the small buildings are intact enough to block the view of what may be inside their deteriorating walls. Quynn points to a piece of cloth sticking to the side of a small building. The boys walk toward it to get a better look.

The cloth is like a blue and red flag, like the combination of two flags. Two different animals stand side to side in the center of the flag, as partners going into battle against some enemy greater to them than each other.

Zerin speaks. "This part is red like the colors of the Arizz. What do the other colors represent?

"The Trett carry a blue flag at times. Perhaps the two were united at one point," suggests Senokre.

"Ha," laughs Lach, "no Arizz warrior would shame themselves so much as to stand side by side with a Trett."

Zerin speaks. "It is possible. There were greater threats in the old days. Perhaps there was a time when the two tribes had to join together."

"There is no threat dangerous enough that I would ever stand with a Trett in battle. The day that the Trett and Arizz join will be my last day on this planet," Lach says defiantly.

Lach stares for a moment at the flag. Angered, he speaks sharply to Zerin and Senokre. "No more speak about this unity, considering that the very tribe you speak of could be waiting over that hill, waiting to separate us from our heads. This flag means nothing, and for all we know it could be some other small group that was destroyed long ago.

Enough about this flag. It is ancient and meaningless."

Lach pauses for a moment then looks at Zerin, as was the way of Lach that even his best friend could be the target of his sarcasm if that friend dare say what he did not agree with, and mockingly says, "Perhaps it is the flag of Salazaar. A wild dream of a man who believes in peace, with a people that want us dead. Salazaar? Salazaar, have you been here? Do you visit when your ridiculous words of peace are not taken seriously in councils with the king and others? Oh Salazaar?"

Zerin ignores the taunt and walks away from the flag so as to avoid any more conflict. Being someone who thought ahead, Zerin knows that it is far too early in this journey to be on bad terms with one another. So he lets it go and upon turning, notices a small building in the back of the fort that has the appearance of having been set ablaze.

"What is that building over there?" he asks.

Zerin walks over to the charred building.

"This building was set ablaze, though none of the others were," says Zerin.

He walks closer to the building and peeks through the cracks in the walls. He stares for a moment then finally realizes what he is looking at inside and he steps away horrified.

"What do you see?" asks Senokre.

Zerin shakes his head, but says nothing and walks away.

"What did you see, Zerin?" asks Quynn.

Zerin does not answer. Lach walks over to a partial door leading into the building. The door is not whole. Whatever fire was upon this door gnawed away at the wood and what is left is held together by the metal used to shape it. Lach forces open the door and the charred remains of the former inhabitants of this fort fall out of the opening, as if they had been waiting by the door for someone to release them.

Lach stares inside. Many more burnt skeletons lay piled on top of each other. Some skeletons are still in a seated position against the walls. There are skeletons of all sizes, including several that are small enough to be children. The other boys look inside. Zerin keeps his distance.

"These skeletons were by the door, like someone piled them there," comments Quynn.

"I do not believe they were piled there by someone, but piled on top of each other, trying to escape the fire. These are not dead bodies set to fire. These people were locked inside and burned alive," states Zerin with a grim look on his face.

"Why?" asks Senokre.

"Because people are evil. Because there will never be peace in this world. Death is all there is and one way or the other, we are destined for it." Quynn states.

"This is a terrible thing. What purpose does it serve to do this to people? Most of these skeletons do not appear to be warriors. What purpose does it serve to kill women and children?" asks a distraught Senokre.

Lach looks around at the boys and speaks. "This is what war is. This is why there can be no peace until the enemy is destroyed. There is evil out there that will do this to the innocent. This is why, when you hear men speak of peace without war, laugh, because there is not such a thing. So let this burn into your minds as the fire burned into their dying bodies, for if you are to be warriors, then you have seen what is to come. This will not be the last atrocity you see, as long as the Trett run freely threatening our very existence. Be prepared."

Lach walks away from the building and continues his speech. "Do not take this from my word alone. I am still young and have many things to experience, but I have learned from Olkar, who has seen many, many wars, that this is the reality of war, and so I am prepared, and so you should be.

Senokre follows Lach who exits the fort. Zerin walks with Quynn a little behind.

"I do not agree with what he said about peace and war," whispers Zerin.

Quynn gives Zerin a look of someone who has experienced great pain recently, which inspires his response. "I do agree with Lach. The Trett are treacherous, and there is no peace in them." Quynn walks away from Zerin.

Zerin takes a moment and looks around the fort once more. He stares at the flag of the united colors and wonders of its history. He glances at the burned building and the charred skeletons that lay at the door. He sighs and follows his friends.

Chapter 3

The boys continue their journey. Not far behind is Juntor, still waiting for the right moment to reveal himself. He glances at the old fort, but it looks far too scary for him to enter alone, so he passes it by, watching it out of the corner of his eye as he walks past.

The day begins to change into night. The shadows grow long and the sun begins to hide behind the trees in the west.

"It is getting dark and we have not reached our first stopping point," says Senokre.

"We spent too long in that old fort," Lach comments.

"We'll need to plan on setting up a campsite pretty soon. I do not wish to see what comes out at night around here, even if we are still in Arizz territory," says Senokre

"Let us go ahead and set up camp here. Maybe it will be a good thing to spend our first night in our own lands," says Zerin.

The boys stop and set up camp. Senokre and Zerin gather up some sticks for firewood. Quynn stands off to the side, staring at the distant mountains, deep in thought. Lach practices his sword play.

Off in the distance, Juntor has realized his first obstacle of the journey. He will have to camp alone, or reveal himself to the boys. Juntor decides that they are not far away enough from the Great City, so he decides to camp alone, but he will get as close to the boys as possible, just in case.

He sets up his camp a few hills away from the others. He makes sure his camp is at the bottom of a hill, so that his fire will be hidden from easy view. When he finishes his campsite, he lays his head on his bag and watches the stars as they slowly appear. He revels in the fact that this is the first time he has been on his own and grows proud in his new independence.

"My father would not be brave enough to go on an adventure like this and camp out under the stars. I will be better than my father. When I have children of my own, I will raise them right, using all that I have learned from my father's mistakes. I will bring honor back to my family's name."

Juntor smiles and throws another piece of wood into the fire. He lays back to continue looking at the stars. The light from the fire flashes on his face showing, as it grows, his new found confidence.

Deep into the night, the stars are out and the moon, half full, creates some shadows on the ground. The four boys sleep in a circle around what is left of their fire. A noise in the distance awakens Lach, who was not in too deep of sleep, because he was dreaming about war, and he was in a very dangerous moment. He sits up and tries to pinpoint the source of the noise. He stands and walks to the peak of the hill where their camp is set. From here Lach realizes he is hearing voices, many voices in the distance, celebrating. He looks around for the direction of the noise and spots, off to the east, a light glow coming from the opposite side of a hill. He watches for a moment, pondering what he should do.

He looks at the three sleeping boys and decides to leave them and go check out the scene for himself. He grabs his sword, slips away and walks toward the ruckus.

The voices are that of a group of nomads, not Trett, nor Arizz. About twenty men and a few women yelling and dancing around a large fire. A few horses stand in the shadows of the campsite. Several men eat meat from some sort of animal and many men drink from large bottles. The men are of a rougher sort than is common in the Great City. They are rougher looking than the Trett, also. Most have beards and are dressed in rags and animal skins. They are very large men, kind of fat actually, and their purpose to Lach is unknown.

Lach watches for a moment, hoping to find some sort of sign that would mark the group as Trett, but there are no markings at all. He sits down, hidden from their view by the darkness and observes. Several of the women do a strange dance, like something they may have learned from watching birds move when they were walking on the ground. Lach is fascinated by this unusual crew.

After a few moments of watching, Lach hears sneaking footsteps behind him. He pretends not to notice, but grasps his sword, ready to strike. A shadow of an image walks near him. Lach can see it out of the corner of his eye. It does not seem to notice him, so Lach sits silent. The shadow stops as if looking at the crowd at the fire. The image looks around and pauses as it looks in Lach's direction. Lach stays frozen and watches the image beside him, daring it, in his mind, to make a move. The unknown creature stares for a bit and Lach decides he has been seen, so he jumps up, sword drawn and lunges at the shadow.

Lach halts his sword just at the chest of the stranger, as he recognizes that it is Juntor. Juntor does not recognize Lach before fright forces a loud scream from deep inside his body. So loud that the people at the fire go silent and begin to look toward the two boy's direction.

Lach and Juntor watch silently as the strange group begins to talk and point. Lach realizes that the shadow of their images can be seen by the moonlight. Several men begin to gather their weapons and many continue to point.

"We must get away. There are far too many for me to take alone. You can explain what you are doing here later, if we should survive you advertisement," Lach says as he pulls Juntor along.

The boys jog back toward their campsite. Juntor has trouble running on the terrain in the dark and slows Lach. The two boys manage to get back to the campsite, where the other three are awake and looking around.

"What is going on? What was that noise?" asks Senokre.

"You heard the yells of Juntor, our new companion, and his first order of business was to make sure that you weren't the only ones who heard. A group of men are chasing us. I do not know of what tribe they are from, but they do not look like any that I am familiar with and they do not look friendly."

"Shall we fight?" ask Senokre.

"I do not believe the five of us can take on the twenty that I saw, or the others that may live in these lands as well," answers Lach.

The noise of shouting men gets closer as the boys gather up the last of their things and hurry along. With the shouts of the men, there is also the barking of dogs. The unfamiliar territory is a disadvantage to the boys and their flight is slow. The barking and shouting gets closer and closer for every hill the boys cross.

"We do not know where we are going. We do not know of a place to hide. This running is futile as they are gaining on us and when they catch us, we will be too exhausted to defend ourselves. We need either to make our stand here or come up with a better plan as we flee," says Quynn.

"Shall we separate? That may confuse the dogs and then maybe we can circle back around and some of us can take them by surprise," suggests Senokre.

"I believe there are too many to battle with. Let us split up and return to their camp and take it by surprise. I may have seen horses. If we can get a few of them, then we can get away," suggests Lach.

"OK, everyone split up," commands Quynn.

The boys run in different directions with the intention

of doing a circle back around. The move does confuse the dogs, as a few try to go one way and the others lead their masters the other way. This confuses the men for a moment and they call a halt to their pursuit.

"Why are your dogs going that way?" asks one man.

"Why do your dogs go that way?" asks another.

"Why does this dog go straight?" asks yet another man, pointing at one of the dogs.

"I only saw two images, yet these dogs act as if they are following several," says the first man.

"Well I don't like that. What was two turns into many. Whether a great army or an evil magic, I do not wish to challenge either," says a man.

"So let us give up this pursuit. If they run, then they are no threat."

"I would still suggest some of us to stand guard throughout the night."

"Very well, then. I am thirsty anyway. We will return to our camp," says the first man.

The men lead their dogs back toward the campsite.

Meanwhile, the four boys run their circle and come back to the group's camp from the opposite side. By luck they join each other and stand just out of view of the fire light, on the edge of the shadows.

"What now?" Senokre asks, just as he notices that Juntor is missing. "Where is Juntor?"

The boys glance around but get no sight of Juntor.

"Maybe he will be back in a moment. He has difficulty running on this terrain," suggests Lach.

The boys lie on their stomachs and watch the remaining people at the camp. The women of the camp are quite ugly, not being too much smaller in size than the men. They sit with the few men who stayed behind and continue to eat and drink and laugh, having already forgotten about the two images from earlier.

Zerin looks occasionally for signs of Juntor. "I am worried about Juntor. He should have returned by now."

"We will wait a few more minutes till we know it is safe and then we will look for him. The night is coming to an end and we will not have the cover of darkness to escape under, so be prepared," Senokre says, as he looks around for Juntor.

The sounds of the men approach the camp. They return laughing and celebrating as if they have earned a victory over the boys tonight. The men come in one by one and sit around the campfire.

"OK, the men have returned and seem to be in no hurry to find us, so let us leave now and look for Juntor.

The boys get up, but Zerin notices something among the people as he stands. He grabs Senokre and points. "They have Juntor."

Among the last of the men to return to the camp, two hold Juntor by the arms and lead him in. Many voices rise as the people take notice of the prize. The women circle Juntor, making noises and laughing. Fear holds Juntor's face, but he fights back his tears.

"What a present you have brought us tonight, a little boy," one woman says as she pokes at Juntor's stomach and pinches at his arm.

The men hand Juntor over to a woman. The woman pulls Juntor to a few other women and they giggle and poke at him.

"He's just right," says one woman.

The boys continue to watch. They are confused as to what the group's intentions are with Juntor.

"I hope they don't eat him," says Quynn.

"Come on!" responds Zerin. "This is no time to joke. We have to figure out how to get him out of there, before they try to marry him to some ugly wench, or adopt him, or brainwash him into some crazy person."

"They probably need some new blood. We better get him out of there before they turn him into one of them," says Lach

"Let's be patient. We will watch out for him and when they go to sleep, we will go free him. For now, we need to wait for the right opportunity. They aren't hurting him and he seems to have the women fascinated. We will wait. What is the worst that could happen?" Senokre asks, while watching the goings on at the camp.

The boys watch as the men begin to build up their fire. The boys see the women rubbing, what appears to them to be some kind of ointment, on Juntor. A few men cut up some vegetables.

"It looks like he is about treated to a feast," says Quynn.

"Maybe they believe he is some sort of higher being and they are going to worship him. They sure do not seem as threatening as they were when they first saw us," says Lach.

The boys continue to watch, amazed and confused. Two men bring out a huge pot and set it over the fire. The pot is filled with water and the cut up vegetables are thrown into it. A woman throws some spices in the water.

"They are actually fixing a meal this big in the middle

of the night? What kind of strange people are these that eat breakfast so early, or dinner so late?" asks Senokre.

"Now I'm asking myself should we attack or should we join the feast?" Quynn says, his stomach growling at the thought of a huge meal. "So shall we go to them in peace? Perhaps they were startled by your image and felt threatened. Perhaps they are good people."

"I do not know," says Zerin. "If you desire to go down there, then go. I am staying up here and I will keep an eye on things."

"I have no intentions of going there, other than to rescue Juntor. So until then, I stay here also," says Lach.

"Well, it is settled. I will go and eat to my heart's content and you can stay and dream about food," Quynn responds to Lach and then looks at Senokre. "What about you?"

Senokre thinks for a moment. He is unsure, but all the talk of food has made him hungry as well. He answers, "I believe I will join you, though I feel we should be more cautious than you seem to be. I am hungry though, so let us see if they will share with us."

Senokre and Quynn stand, prepared to walk to the camp site.

Lach and Zerin jump up and draw their swords. Zerin speaks, "You do not want to eat of what they are planning on cooking."

Senokre and Quynn look toward the camp. The women are now sprinkling spices over Juntor's body. The same spices they were sprinkling in the pot. The women begin stuffing pieces of vegetables into Juntor's clothes and they wrap a string of onions around his neck.

Quynn's eyes get very big and he speaks. "I told you! I told you they were going to eat him!"

"You told us?" Counters Lach. "You were just about to join in."

"We must make some noise and distract the people," says Senokre.

"Draw your swords, Arizz warriors, we are about to do battle, and this is not a drill," Lach says, as a leader would say just before battle. "I will tell you this that I have learned from Olkar. The first kill will wound our hearts and we will feel remorse, and we will never be the same. But we are warriors, in a time of war, and we have no other choice. Kill all who threaten you and do not hesitate, or it will be you that is killed."

The boys make a lot of noise. The people of the camp are distracted and look, momentarily stopping their meal plans.

Lach raises his sword and yells, "first kill, attack!"

The boys, timid in expression but bold in approach, march on the camp. Many of the men hold their swords at the ready.

"Who goes there?" asks one man.

Still in the shadows and out of sight, Lach shouts in response. "Free the boy and flee from this area and you shall not face our wrath."

One of the men laughs. "By the pitch of your voice, you are either a boy yourself or his mother, who has come to rescue him."

Lach responds defiantly, as Lach consistently did. He had the heart of a warrior as well as the words of one. "Be careful not to judge your opponent by the sound of his voice, but rather by the edge his sword, if your body will allow you to do so, before it falls to the ground to become a rotting carcass."

The men look around at each other and one speaks. "Show yourself hard warrior with the soft voice, for words are easily spoken as old men and young children also have strong use of their tongues yet no strength to wield a sword."

Lach is insulted and of course moves out from the shadows, showing himself. The men and women laugh.

"Another little boy. Now we have two nights of meals ahead of us," a woman says.

"What do you want little boy with a big mouth? You desire to save you friend, yet you will only join him. Give up your sword now and surrender peacefully. I do not wish to have the blood of a child upon my sword," says a man.

"Not upon your sword, but in your belly, hey Sren?" asks another man.

The other three boys stay in the shadows giving the appearance that Lach is the only threat. Lach looks around at the group of large men, assessing the situation. Lach knows there are just too many for the boys to fight in all out battle, so he comes up with an idea.

"So you see a boy in front of you? No threat, just another meal. Then perhaps a meal is best won through a little competition than just given up freely," says Lach.

"What do you mean, boy?" asks Sren.

"Though I am young, I am a trained warrior, from a bloodline of great warriors. Upon looking at you with you fat bellies and your unshaven faces and your unpleasant women, which I see there are few, I see lazy sluggish sloths, who would fall at my feet after only a few unsuccessful swipes of their own swords. I challenge your best warriors, one by one. If I can defeat your best warriors, then you will return my friend. Do not fret at the possibility of losing your meal. I believe you may consider skipping a few if you survive this night."

"I hear your brazen words and I no longer have pity for your youth, for someone chose to spare the rod, and now a spoiled child stands in front of us. We accept your challenge and it is too bad that in death you will learn the lessons that should have been taught to you already," responds Sren.

Lach grips his sword tightly and speaks to himself. "If you only knew the lessons that I have been taught."

Sren calls over a very large man, larger than the rest of the large men, though they all are very similar in appearance. This one appears younger and stronger.

"This is Wren, my son. He is our greatest warrior. Let not yourself judge him by his fat belly and unshaven face, for you may awaken in the afterworld, after learning such a lesson."

Wren draws his sword and smirks at Lach. Lach takes his fighting stance and observes the situation. This is the first real time that Lach will fight to the death. He has had many practice battles with swords, but never has he had to finish his opponent as he will have to now.

Lach draws on all the lessons taught to him by his mentor, Olkar. He is aware that a real fight has nothing of the feeling as it does in practice. While the same skills will be utilized, the feelings, deep in the soul are different. It is of hate and fear, where even the victor doesn't come away unscarred, whether on the skin or in the soul, the scars will always remain. But, in a time of war, what other options do men have?

Lach circles Wren, observing his opponents movement, searching for weaknesses. Wren watches with overconfidence as the boy circles him. Wren feints a few lunges at Lach, taunting him.

"Make your attack little warrior, so that I may finish you and we can have our meal," Wren says and then glances at Sren with a smirk.

Lach sees the look and lunges in at Wren, just missing piercing the expanded belly of the large man. Wren stumbles in surprise and then regains his composure. Lach takes up his battle stance again.

"He almost got you there Wren," says one man laughing.

Wren frowns at Lach and steps forward, swiping his sword at the boy. Lach blocks the attack with his sword, but realizes immediately the power that comes from such a huge man. The impact jars though Lach's body and he steps back to regain his control. Wren attacks again. This time Lach dodges the attack and moves out of harm's way. Wren stumbles forward after the miss and where size creates power, it also takes a lot of energy to control a large body and Wren's face shows his overexertion. Lach fakes an attack on Wren, forcing Wren to be defensive, then Lach steps to the side, throwing Wren's balance off again.

"Be still little rabbit, so that I may show you what a real warrior is," says Wren.

Lach immediately attacks Wren with several hard and fast shots of his sword, forcing Wren to move in defense much faster than the robust man wants to. When the attack is complete, Lach steps back. The behemoth now breathes heavily and he doesn't hold his sword quiet as high.

"Surrender now and I will not kill you in front of your father. Though I do not like him, and he may be my next victim, either way," challenges Lach.

Wren does not like the threat to his father and charges at Lach. Lach dodges a few swipes of Wren's sword, but is forced to block a few and they take their toll, knocking Lach backwards onto the ground. He scrambles to get up, expecting Wren to go in for the kill, but Wren does not. The obese warrior stands, bent over with his hands on his knees, panting. Lach moves toward Wren.

"Stand straight and face your executioner," Lach commands.

Wren waves his hand as if asking for a time out. Lach pauses for a moment, confused.

"Do you surrender? If you do then release my friend, or send out another warrior, for your first offering was very disappointing," responds Lach

"This fight is to the death. Do not attempt to get out of it so cowardly," says Sren. "In a moment, my son will prepare you for the pot."

Lach is confused. Though he is a warrior, he is young and slow at finding answers to this unusual situation that he is not familiar with. He pauses for a moment then reality hits him.

"Raise your sword, this fight must have an end," Lach demands.

"Be patient boy, I must catch my breath first."

"There is no pause in a battle to the end. Surrender and release my friend now! Do you surrender?"

"I do not surrender to you …"

Before Wren can finish his words, Lach attacks him while he is still bent over and stabs the sword through his back. The force of the strike knocks Wren to the ground and Lach's sword binds him to the ground as a nail in a coffin. Lach struggles, but pulls the sword out and looks over his first kill in uncomfortable glory.

Several women scream. Sren runs over to his deceased son. Several men begin to rumble amongst themselves. Sren holds Wren in his arms and when he sees that his son is dead, lets out a horrific yell. While Sren looks upon his dead child, Lach looks back toward the edge of the fire light toward his friends with anguish in his eyes then turns back to Sren.

"Release my friend!" commands Lach with a crack in his voice as he takes a battle stance. "I will kill you all if I have to."

A large older man, Hrun, seeming to be of some importance, steps forward. "Be gone with you, evil little warrior. You have killed this poor man's only child. Leave us to mourn his death and so that we may forget your dastardly deed."

Lach is confused by the verbal assault. Did this man and his entire tribe not just intend on eating Juntor? How is killing someone doing a bad thing worse than eating an innocent child? In his youthful mind, Lach ponders these unusual circumstances. Being the first time that Lach had ever dealt with irrational people, Lach searches for the proper answer with no avail.

"You are angered that I defeated your kin, yet you expect not that I be angered by your intentions with mine?" asks Lach.

"Your kin, that boy is our prize. We got him fair and square," chimes in Hrun. "You killed out of anger. We only need the young man for food. We are a starving people. How would you deny us our right to eat?"

"Juntor is not an animal, which we all use for food. He is a human. You cannot eat a human," responds Lach, now completely caught off guard by these people's mindset. Lach stares for a moment, amazed at this group. Lach expression turns to anger as the warrior in him focuses back on the mission at hand. "Release my friend, now!"

The people look at Lach with amazement. It seems that they are as confused by his mindset as he is of theirs. Hrun chimes in again. "Why do you continue to threaten us? Please leave. You have done your evil, now go."

"Release our friend," shouts a voice from the shadows. The people look toward Zerin, Quynn, and Senokre as they move into view. "Release our friend, and stop with your games," commands Quynn.

"Now there are more of you? Do you also come to do some evil to a poor and downtrodden people?" shouts Hrun.

Sren stands up beside his son's body and speaks. "You have killed one of our people. You now owe us. We will keep your friend as payment. Now that we are even, you may go."

Lach looks at Quynn, now hoping that the oldest of the boys would take over the negotiation. Quynn stares at the people with the same amazement and confusion that Lach has.

"You took our friend before your man was killed. Your man was killed because you took our friend. We owe you nothing, and you must return our friend, for you are the evil doers if you eat him," says Quynn.

Sren goes and stands beside Hrun while many of the women mourn over Wren's body. Sren speaks. "You must all leave now. This is our camp and we do not welcome intruders." Sren begins to get hysterical. "Leave at once you foul beings. We do not welcome you here and asks that you leave so that we may stay our swords."

Lach does not like this threat and his warrior nature takes over his confusion as Zerin tries to speak to the people. "He is only a child. Surely as different as our cultures may be, we are not so different in the protection of an innocent child?"

"It was a child that just murdered my son. Any friend of that child is not worthy of such a label, as innocent," says Sren.

Zerin is about to speak again, but is interrupted as Lach races toward Sren. Before Sren can react, Lach swipes his sword at Sren's neck and Sren's head flops to the ground as his body poses for a minute, still responding to the head's last command then follows it to the ground. The women scream. Lach resets himself prepared to strike again and speaks, "No more talk! For every minute that Juntor is imprisoned another head shall fly. No matter if you are man, woman or child." Lach looks toward a woman holding a baby. The woman cowers back.

"You are a murderer. You have now killed two of our people," says Hrun.

"I'll kill you all if you do not obey my commands. It will be best for these lands if I do so," says Lach.

A fat woman steps forward, named Yiri, and speaks. "Please leave us. We are hungry and desire to eat and be at peace. You have caused enough pain for us that it will take many months to get over. Please leave, foul children of the dark, go back to your dark corners and evil tribe."

Before Yiri finishes her words, Lach, who had been looking at her while she spoke, turns with a flash, sword wielded and chops off the head of Hrun, who stands beside her. Hrun's head flies into some of the people and they scream.

Zerin, Senokre and Quynn watch the events unfold, unsure of what they should do. Lach stands back in his offensive position readying for his next strike.

"Now you must ask yourself, who is next, who will feel my wrath?" Lach states boldly then looks at a younger man standing close by. "You? Will it be you?" A young man named Treb looks in amazement as Lach continues, "Well, will it? Do you want to feel my wrath?"

The people of the tribe stare with blankness in their faces, as if Lach has been speaking in a foreign tongue and that all he said made no sense to them. They still do not understand that all they have to do is release Juntor and the boys would leave.

Quynn recognizes this and instead of continuing with the futile negotiation, walks to where Juntor is held. The people watch Quynn, unsure of the obvious. Zerin watches Quynn while Senokre watches Lach, realizing that another strike may be coming.

"Where does he go?" one of the tribesmen ask.

Quynn arrives at the spot where two women hold Juntor captive. Quynn nudges his way to Juntor, who lies on his back, and helps him up. The women stare in shock. The men watch, but with no action. Quynn unties Juntor and they walk back to Zerin and Senokre.

A woman shouts, "They are stealing our food!"

Lach tightens his grip on his sword intending on striking again. Senokre notices and chimes in. "Lach, we have Juntor. We can leave now. Lach does not heed the words of his friend and stares with rage at his next intended victim.

"Lach?" calls Quynn.

Zerin walks over to Lach and places his hand on his shoulder. Lach does not respond.

"It is OK Lach. Juntor is safe and these people are no longer a threat," says Zerin.

Lach relaxes his grip on his sword and his body loses its rigid battle form. He looks at Zerin then the two join the other boys and they exit the small campsite. Moans and screams wail up in the background as the people of the tribe tend to their dead. The boys walk away victorious, but confused by the events that just unfolded.

Lach keeps some distance from the rest of the boys so that they will not see the pain in his face and the tears in his eyes.

Chapter 4

The midday sun shines high in the sky with a few small clouds dotting the sky like pieces of cotton stuck to a blue canvas. It creates a beautiful day, bringing about a feeling of happiness, far from the actual mood of the boys now several hours away from their first major obstacle on this adventure.

They study the landscape of this new area, now being far enough away from familiar lands, to see new and exciting terrains. The Pryon Mountains have grown as the distance between the boys and the towering landmark has shrunk. The rolling hills are now getting smaller and further behind them as they venture into flatlands like a shallow valley. The area is covered by tall grass that flows in the wind. There are few trees, but the trees that are present have wide outstretched branches, covered with large leaves creating a canopy of relief from today's relentless sun.

The boys pass under one of these trees and Senokre speaks up. "What say we take a rest here for a while? We have hiked a good ways and I did not get all the sleep I require after last night's run in with the crazies."

"I agree," says Quynn. "Our rest was cut short by the excitement and I do not wish to encounter any more of it, lest I be rested to take on a challenge in this unfamiliar place."

The boys agree, even Lach who had the most excitement of the night and of course Juntor who finds a place under the tree on some tall grass. He makes it into a nice bed and falls fast asleep.

Senokre too, finds a good spot to lie on and after a few moments of looking at the sun drenched valley, he can no longer fight the battle with his eyelids and he closes them for a long nap.

Lach, Zerin and Quynn sit at the edge of the shadow of the tree looking much like three elders trying to have wise council on their next intended actions.

"Maybe we should turn back. That was too close of a call for Juntor back there. I do not know how much more dangerous this journey will become, but I expect the further we get from our homes, it will become more and more dangerous. And Juntor now being on this adventure, he is far too young to journey with us." Zerin says, looking mostly to his closest friend, knowing that no matter what anyone else says Lach's decisions are final.

"He is the youngest of us, but we are all only children as compared to what is considered an adult. I believe this will be a good learning experience for him, as it will be for us," comments Quynn.

"I agree. Though we are viewed as children, we are still Arizz warriors and this will be a good training exercise to help us be more prepared for battle in the future," says Lach.

"I am with you two then. I just feel responsible for Juntor, you know, with his bad home life. But we are warriors first and any time away from his father is probably safer than being at home," says Zerin.

The boys nod in agreement and sit silent for a few moments looking out over the vast new land. A slight sign of pride shows in their faces, as a young man begins his steps to independence, a boy progressing toward becoming a man.

The shadow of the tree now covers the ground, extending outward on one side and shrinking on the other as the sun begins its exit for the day. All the boys now sleep under the shade. Even though they are on their way to growing up, they are still boys and a good nap is impossible to resist.

So the boys sleep most of the remainder of the day, reviving their energy sources. Though not planned out, a good strategy by accident since they will need all the strength they can muster for what lies ahead.

On the edge of dark with a partial moon slowly taking on its share of the responsibility of lighting the night, Senokre is the first to wake. He looks around at his friends. He looks out across the land then gets up to stretch his legs. His stirring wakes the ever on guard Lach, who gets up and joins him.

"It is late. We have slept away the day and I do not know if it would be wise to travel at night," says Lach.

"We need a tree like this near the city. I would take a nap every day after school," says Senokre.

"A tree like this would make a warrior lazy, and the Trett would surely take the kingdom," responds Lach.

"Maybe we should plant some trees like this near the Trett colony, and let their warriors become lazy, and the absolute victory can be ours," jokes Senokre.

"That would be too easy. We would not have a good war and that would be boring to have an easy victory," answers Lach.

Senokre looks on Lach, studying his meaning through what his face is saying then asks, "Wouldn't it be better to have an easy victory, so we can have a faster peace?"

"Peace makes warriors weak. There will always be some evil, somewhere, just waiting for that moment. Whether by war or squashing a small rebellion, it is good to have some sort of battle going on. People are weak and easily swayed by evil influence. It only takes one snake tongued fool to turn hundreds to his evil cause. People need to be controlled," answers Lach.

"But who will control them?" asks Senokre.

"The most powerful, of course," answers Lach.

"What if an evil man is the most powerful?" asks Senokre.

"You see an evil man will never have control over the people, because he will do evil to them and many will not stand for it. So however many rebellions he crushes, the people will be reminded of his evil done upon them, because he will continue to do evil to them, and they will always stand against him and eventually he will lose."

"Why would this not apply to a good man as well?" asks Zerin who has joined the conversation.

"Because to control the people through evil is evil and good will always stand against it. A good man will rule through force, allowing the people to live in peace as long as they conform to his rules," answers Lach.

"People feel deep in their soul that they have certain rights and will not stand for freedoms being taken away. How do you propose to control that?" asks Zerin.

"Make the people comfortable in their situation and slowly take away their rights, as you call it. They will conform. To keep an ounce of their common convenience they will give up most of their rights. People generally do not want conflict, so give them peace and they will give you their freedom. And those who rebel will be squashed. Unlike the rule of an evil man, there will be less rebellion. They just don't want to deal with it," answers Lach.

"And you, what would you do if your rights were taken?" asks Zerin.

"I would conquer those that attempted to take my rights."

"And if you can't?" asks Zerin.

"Then I will die fighting for my freedom?" answers Lach. "I do not say I agree with this philosophy, but it will work best. Eventually all the strong willed will be extinct, except one and he will be the leader."

"There is a lot of blood in your plan," Zerin says.

"Better to die fighting to be free than live as a prisoner in your own life. The weak will accept this, because they are weak. The strong will not and will die fighting or be the one to rise to power," says Lach.

"I believe people are wise enough to make their own decisions. I believe we will not always agree with others, but I believe that people have a right to be free and left alone as long as they do not hurt other innocent people. Live and let live," comments Zerin.

"Oh how your father does speak through you," ridicules Lach.

"Actually my friend, my father and you would seem to be more in agreement, as he believes that more control of people is necessary," responds Zerin

Lach frowns at Zerin's comment and becomes aggravated. "I guarantee you that I, in no way, see eye to eye with your father."

Zerin looks at Senokre with a smirk and says, "I don't know. It sounded very similar to the conversation we had the other night at dinner."

Senokre catches on to Zerin's attempt to pick at Lach and snickers. Lach is offended and stomps away.

"He will be a great warrior one day," says Senokre.

"A great warrior yes, but if he ever becomes a leader, I fear he may be more dreaded than The General. He will have no mercy on those who stand against him and his grudges will be long and his wrath will be severe. If the Arizz win this war with the Trett and Lach gets his way, we may be only trading one bloodthirsty tyrant for another." Zerin makes his comment as he watches Lach swinging his sword, practicing perhaps or perhaps swinging out of rage then says, "I am going to sleep some more, since it is night already."

Senokre watches Zerin walk away then glances toward Lach. Senokre is puzzled by the two who are so very different yet in many ways are exactly the same. He watches Lach continue to mimic battle, admiring the young warrior's talents. Finally laying down he looks at the stars till his eyes close.

Senokre lies in the same spot, sleeping in peace, forgetting about all the dangers ahead. The sun begins to spread its light all about and upon Senokre's face, trying to disturb his sleep, but is beaten to the task by Lach who stands over him.

"Wake young warrior. We have wasted half a day yesterday, and I do not intend on wasting any more time," Lach says as he stares off into the distance.

Senokre gets up slowly, like he was awakened during a deep sleep, and wipes his eyes and looks around. The other boys are awake and are eating or gathering up their things.

"I want us to reach that small forest over there," says Lach as he points across the great river basin to a patch of woods that lie beyond, under the shadow of the Pryon Mountains. "I believe we can make good time across this flat land."

Quynn joins Lach and asks, "Why have you set your goal for those woods?"

"I believe if there are any trees as good as this one we slept under, then a good night's rest awaits us, and a good reward motivates warriors to move quickly. Yes, we can make it to those trees by night," answers Lach.

So the boys ready themselves and set out across the grassy, flat land. Lach leads the way, being it his nature to lead, followed by Senokre then Quynn. Zerin and Juntor follow from behind. There is pride in the boys' faces. They are coming of age and they are on an adventure like one that only a few of the bravest have ever been on. Juntor's face can hardly contain his excitement as he walks with a huge grin. He is free of his father and feels he must be impressing his hero, Zerin. He is determined to prove himself, and sometime on this adventure, he intends on doing just that.

The journey across the grassy plain is calm as they had hoped. The time passes quickly due to the unfamiliar scenery that the boys observe during their walk, making them forget about hours and minutes.

They see little birds, unlike those they had seen back home. Very small birds, which seem to never stop flapping their wings. They eat from flowers without stopping and weave in and out from each other, as if in some sort of conversation using dance instead of words.

Juntor stumbles over a small stone because he is so amused by the bird, but catches himself before he falls and looks embarrassingly to the other boys to see if his clumsy step was seen. Luckily no one saw and his face quickly comes back to life with his excited smile.

The boys come upon a small river in the center of the flat land. It is very wide, but shallow. It is like a resting point for the waters after having come raging down the steep edges of the high hills and mountains. The water is calm and relaxed and gives home to fish that can be seen swimming here and there tending to their business.

The boys stop for a break, filling their water bottles from the shallow river. They find a small tree with just enough shade for the five of them to sit.

"I wish I lived here," says Juntor. "There are so many different and amazing things all around."

"This is very beautiful place, but we are too far away from our own people for it to be a safe place to live, especially with The General still trying to take over the kingdom," answers Quynn.

"I would not live here because it would bring me too far away from that tyrant. I intend on being the one to slay the evil traitor and I would want to be closest to his reign of terror," Lach says, not in a boisterous way, but as one who has every bit of his intention set on doing such a deed.

"Danger is everywhere, whether far from our people or anywhere near the Trett army, but today, right now is peace. Can we forget about what awaits us at home and can we forget what our destiny may hold and just for this moment enjoy this peaceful place? I am sure that if this is not Aragopia itself, then I will hope that Aragopia is very similar. I fear that what truly does lie ahead for us is danger and war, whether on this adventure or when we get back home. I would like to enjoy this moment for now, because it may be our one and only time for such a feeling," Zerin says with wisdom in his voice.

Senokre speaks up. "I like this place also. Why do we not, once we are older, get some people together and establish a colony here? With enough people we can have the numbers to protect ourselves from the Trett or any other threat."

"There are many other threats than just the Trett that many of our people have never heard of. Perhaps there are things more dangerous than the Trett and The General beyond the lands that we are familiar with," says Quynn.

Lach looks at Senokre and says. "Don't get caught up in Zerin's dream of peace and happiness. We must always be ready for any danger that may arise."

"You speak of all the bad things that we have never heard of. There is just as much possibility of good things in these lands that we have never heard of either. Like this Aragopia we are searching for, perhaps there are other good people and good things yet to be discovered," answers Zerin.

"Perhaps there is only war and perhaps there is only peace. For now though I agree with Zerin. Let us enjoy this moment and talk of other things, besides war," says Quynn.

The boys sit silent for a moment taking in their surroundings. Lach decides to let go of war for that moment and opens his eyes to the beauty that exists, whether there is war taking place or not.

The boys watch the shallow river as its water slowly journeys on. Occasionally a small pop like the breaking of a twig overtakes the silence for a moment and the calm of the water is disturbed by a fish under it, snapping at a bug that floats on top. The smoothness disturbed by ripples that go their separate ways trekking across the water until they disappear and all is calm again.

A slight breeze blows through and rides the high grass. The few trees here and there rustle as if shivering from a chill. To the north, the white capped mountains sit in the background like a mighty being overlooking its creation and below it, the top of a forest far away, like a green sea of leaves flowing over the top of an abyss of unknown layers below. A vast open area of tall grass lies between there and the shallow river, where the boys now pause.

Lach is amazed by the undisturbed land. Perhaps the boys are the first people to ever have stepped foot on this utopian like terrain. Surely though, Lach thinks, others have ventured through here, perhaps in search of Aragopia or perhaps to get away from war. But no one is settled here and surely, unless there is a foul creature or a dangerous threat lurking nearby, one would have set out to settle this land if they had only seen it in a picture. And if there is a threat, it had not shown itself and the boys were over half a day's journey into it with no sign of danger.

Lach ask his friends. "Do you think we are the first to come to this land? Have we discovered an undiscovered country?"

"We should claim it and name it, if that is so," says Juntor.

"Surely people have been here before," says Quynn.

"But where are they? If they came through here, then they would feel as we do and settled here," asks Lach.

"Maybe they were looking for Aragopia and with the promises of such a land, they passed on these," says Senokre.

"For someone to pass this land up, they surely must have found Aragopia because that is the only reason that someone would not want to live here," says Quynn.

"Perhaps we are closer to Aragopia than we realize, or closer than many who have tried to come in search of the mythical land," says Zerin.

"I hope they found Aragopia and not their fate at the hands of one of these creatures we have been told stories about. Maybe instead of Aragopia, they found a Fikron," says Lach, spoiling their hopeful thoughts.

"Only you would hope to find a Fikron, Lach," says Zerin.

"Let's make up a song for our adventure," chimes in Juntor.

"Song? I'll leave the singing to the women," says

Quynn.

The boys laugh, including Juntor who then speaks up. "You can laugh, but I am going to make up a song for this adventure. Stories are easily remembered in song, and songs last forever so we will be remembered forever.

Lach looks at Juntor with a smile and says, "You better worry about surviving this journey, because songs created aren't heard if the creator never returns to sing them."

Lach stands and stretches his arms. "We have been here long enough. I believe we need to move on so that we may reach that forest by night."

Quynn agrees. "Yeah, we must move on. Don't let this peaceful place make you forget that there is most likely danger ahead."

The boys stand and ready themselves to journey on. They wade through the shallow river. The water comes up only to their waists. Lach leads.

"Be careful not to run into any deep holes that may be hidden under this water, Lach," says Quynn.

The boys cross the calm waters with no trouble and come out on the other side and continue heading toward the forest.

The day is coming to an end. The shadows of the boys stretch long and thin to their sides. The sun paints the sky a dark orange on the horizon like a blazing inferno far to the west.

The boys come upon the small forest that lay in front of the Pryon mountains. The trees are spread thinly so that light is allowed in, even as the sun sets. They pause at the edge of the forest to evaluate their next steps.

"Shall we setup camp here or venture a little further in?" asks Quynn.

Lach answers as he looks back toward the flatlands just crossed. "I think we should go deeper so that we may have some coverage. To sleep on this edge, leaves us open to any evil that may be present in this area."

So the boys agree to travel further into the forest and continue on into the wooded land. As they travel on, they are impressed by the tranquility of the forest. Many different types of trees make up the landscape. Tall thin trees, like pine trees rise up to the very top of the canopy. There are large trees with thick trunks and many branches extending out to others of the same breed as if holding hands or protecting the smaller trees from rain or storm with a shelter of leaves. On the ground, like a crackling carpet, are dry leaves strewn all about. Where leaves do not dominate, grass grows like patches of green hair nurtured by the sun that has been allowed in through openings in the awning of foliage.

Birds sing their last few songs before it is time for them to rest. An occasional rustle in the trees makes a soft noise like a fan blowing on a warm summer night. The pleasant sounds of the forest quickly begin to entice the already drained boys to make camp before they fall asleep where they stand.

The boys fight their eyes, which now feel like their lids are being pulled down by some massive weight from under the ground.

Finally Quynn stops and yawns and says, "I say we make camp here. I fear, if we do not, that I may walk, in a sleep, right into some deep well or dangerous pit."

So the boys all agree and set up their camp. And

though they are unsure of their new surroundings, their fatigue conquers all worry and they all are into deep sleep soon after laying down to rest.

Deep into the night the moon floats in the sky, partially visible from inside the forest. A few stars here and there dot the heavens where the tops of the trees permit. All is silent except for an occasional noise of those animals that are active during the night.

Quynn wakes up from his slumber with a jolt and shouts, "father?" Quynn realizes he has awakened from a dream and sits up looking into the sky. After a while he begins to cry. He cries for a moment until one of the boys stir and Quynn quickly regains his composure and wipes his eyes. He looks around to see if anyone has seen this, but everyone is asleep. He takes a deep breath, raises his hand to the sky then lies back down and closes his eyes.

Juntor slyly opens his eyes and watches Quynn. Having just witnessed Quynn's emotion, he wonders what it was all about and why did he say father? Juntor lays for a moment pondering over what he had just seen, but once again his need for rest overpowers him and he falls back to sleep.

Chapter 5

The sun shines brightly through the loosely arranged trees of the forest. The sun creeps over Juntor's sleeping eyes as if signaling him to wake up. He wakes up to see the other boys gathering their things and preparing for the next leg of the journey. He glances at Quynn, who seems happy and very different than the young man who cried under the stars during the night.

He gets up and stretches and speaks to Zerin who is closest to him. "You guys let me sleep too late. I will hold us up for our leave because I still have to gather my things."

"We are in no hurry, Juntor," answers Zerin.

Juntor pauses to think for a moment then speaks again to Zerin. "What ever happened to Quynn's father? I missed the first leg of this journey and haven't heard if he had gotten better after his injury."

Zerin thinks for a moment and answers. "You know Juntor, I do not know. Our journey started so quickly I have forgotten to ask. I do not believe he has spoken to the others about it, for I believe someone would have told me. No, I believe it has slipped all our minds. I hope Quynn is not insulted by our lack of inquiry. Perhaps he has chosen not to talk about it, but I do not know what that would mean. He chose to come on our trip, when before he said no because of his father's condition. I would take that to mean his father is getting better."

"It would seem that way to me also, except last night I heard him awaken and say father and then cry for a moment before going back to sleep," says Juntor.

"I do not know. I would like to know, but I guess he may tell us how things are going when he is good and ready. I guess then we should not bother him about it. He will tell us when he feels the time is right," answers Zerin.

Juntor gathers his things and after a small meal the boys begin their journey deeper into the forest. They head north using the snow covered peaks of the Pryon Mountains as their marker. After about half a day's journey the boys notice a clearing to the east and some movement.

"There is something moving in that clearing over there," says Senokre.

The boys pause and try to focus in on the thing or things that has caught Senokre's eye. They spy some more movement and kneel to the ground so as not to be seen by whatever creature lurks in the opening.

"What is it?" asks Juntor.

"I cannot tell from here, but it seems to be very large," says Quynn.

"Could it be a Fikron?" asks Juntor.

"I believe Fikrons are black. This creature seems to have some yellow or orange coloring," says Senokre.

"Well, whether it be an evil creature or a good creature, I'd like to know. I do not wish to continue this journey looking over my shoulder with a mysterious creature lurking. I would rather be prepared. I say we sneak closer to see what it is," says Lach.

"I agree. I'd rather know what it is now, rather than be surprised later," agrees Zerin.

So the boys, using all the stealth that they had been trained, slowly work their way closer to the opening. As they get closer, they can see that there are at least two of these strange creatures. As the boys reach the edge of the trees they see just what it is that has drawn their attention. At a tree that stands by itself away from the other trees is a tall, lanky creature with long legs like a horse, but much longer. The body leads up to a very long neck where the head of the creature sits, at least fifteen feet in the air eating leaves out of the top of the tree. It is a yellowish color with brown patches all about its body. Of course it is a giraffe, but the boys had never seen nor heard of such a creature and they kneel in their spots watching in amazement.

A noise draws the boy's attention to more giraffes. They have wandered upon a herd of the lanky creatures that make their home in this land below the Pryon Mountains.

"What are they, Zerin?" asks Juntor.

"I do not know. I have never seen such an animal," answers Zerin.

"They do not look dangerous, but if they are, I believe it would be hard to slay them with their heads being so high off the ground," says Lach.

"Let us watch them for a while and maybe we can learn if we have anything to fear from them," suggests Quynn.

The boys watch the giraffes for about an hour. They see them mostly eating, but a few youngsters play to the side. They seem to communicate with each other through some sort of speech, but the boys do not understand the dialect. After some time the giraffes seem to finish up their business and as a group, slowly wander further and further out of sight.

"Shall we follow? I am very curious to find out more about these creatures," Senokre asks as he strains to get a last glimpse of the animals as they go out of sight.

"I believe we should continue on our journey. We do not know how long it will take and we do not know how much time we can waste on other ventures," says Quynn.

The boys agree and again face north but stay along the edge of the forest opening, hoping to catch another glimpse of the giraffes or any other new creature that may dwell in these parts.

They journey for a few more hours with Lach at the lead. Suddenly he stops in his tracks and raises his hand to warn the others to stop. The boys kneel and Quynn and Zerin scramble up beside Lach.

"What is it?" asks Quynn.

Lach points ahead. "If you look right through there, I believe there is some sort of wall like structure." Lach looks at Zerin. "Do you see it?"

Quynn and Zerin stare through the woods.

"I believe I see it," says Quynn. "It does seem to be some sort of wall."

"Let's get a closer look, but be very careful. I do not wish to come across anymore crazy people like those before," says Zerin.

Lach leads the boys slinking and crawling through and around the trees and the underbrush until they get close enough to see a long wall surrounding something still unseen. The boys edge right up within fifty feet of the wall and pause.

Lach whispers to Quynn. "It looks like a small fort."

The boys observe the scene for a moment. The wall is made up of thin trees tied together side by side, cut to make the wall about ten feet high. Along the outskirts of the wall are small pits, partially covered by branches and debris to disguise them to potential victims.

"It feels as if many eyes are upon us right now," says Lach.

As the boys sit, there is an occasional rustle here and there. The boys catch glimpses of something in the corners of their eyes, but by the time they turn to look, whatever it was is gone.

"I do not believe we are safe here," says Quynn.

"It seems we are surrounded. We should pull our swords and be ready. There may be a battle for us at hand," says Lach.

The boys gather together standing in battle formation and draw their swords. Suddenly the forest comes alive with rustling from all around, like small creatures scurrying all about. The boys look side to side trying to pinpoint the sources of the noises.

"Are they getting closer or are they running away?"

asks Senokre.

Suddenly a squeal, like that of a struggling creature comes from near the wall.

"What is that?" asks Zerin.

The stressed squeal continues, like a distress signal of an injured animal.

"It is coming from over there," Zerin says as he points toward a section of the wall.

The boys stare for a moment and realize the noise is coming from one of the small pits dug near the wall.

"It is coming from one of those pits," says Lach.

"It sounds as if it is injured. Should we help it?" asks Zerin.

"All the noise we heard was made by more than one, so let its kind help it," says Lach.

"I believe it would have been helped by now if its kind was going to help. I am going to go see what it is. I cannot listen to it suffer any longer," says Zerin.

Zerin slowly and cautiously works his way toward the small pit. All the way he walks with sword drawn, looking this way and that for any surprise attack. Zerin arrives at the pit which is set right next to the wall and carefully peeks over the edge.

The pit is about six feet deep and about six feet around. As Zerin peers further over the edge, he sees an unusual creature which is now quiet, having become aware of Zerin's approach.

The creature is a Chimihog, a small furry creature, like a small bear, but it has hands and feet. It is about three feet tall. Though its body is furry, its face has no hair, but is a dark brown color with a snout similar to a pig and a face similar to a monkey or ape. For a moment Zerin and the Chimihog stare at each other, unsure of what to think.

"Are you OK little fellow?" asks Zerin.

The Chimihog stares at Zerin. Zerin stares for another moment then looks around for something to help the creature out. He spies a small dead tree limb, gets it and lowers it into the hole for the Chimihog to use as a ladder to climb out. The Chimihog stares motionless at the limb then at Zerin then at the limb again.

"Come on little friend. Use this to climb out," says Zerin.

The other boys watch from a distance, trying to figure out what Zerin has found. They stand now and whistle, trying to get his attention.

Zerin backs away from the hole and looks back at his friends. He holds up his hand to signal to the boys to stay where they are. When Zerin gets far enough away, he pauses and watches. For a moment there is nothing then suddenly the top of the limb wiggles and slowly the Chimihog climbs out of its accidental trap and stands on the edge, staring at Zerin and the boys.

"What is it?" ask Juntor.

The Chimihog notices Juntor and watches him with curiosity. Juntor returns the fascination and stares at the little creature. It slowly walks toward the wall with a waddling stride, all along staring at the boys, mostly Juntor.

Suddenly an unseen door in the wall opens and two larger Chimihogs walk out to greet the smaller one. The little one is comforted by the female looking Chimihog. All three walk back through the door and it closes behind them.

Zerin looks to the boys and shrugs his shoulders. He is

startled by a noise behind him. He turns to see that a small peephole sized opening has appeared in the wall. An eye peeks through. It appears to be a human eye, and not the dark eye of a Chimihog. Zerin stares at the new mystery.

"Hello?" Zerin speaks.

The eye in the wall looks at Zerin then glances at the other boys then back at Zerin.

"You look like children," says a voice.

"We are," answers Zerin.

"Where are your parents?" asks the voice.

"Our parents are back in our homeland," answers Zerin.

"Why are you here?" asks the voice.

"We were on a journey when we heard the creature's distress and we came to help it," answers Zerin. "May I ask you, who you are?"

The voice pauses for a moment then answers. "I am, uh, Nork."

"I am Zerin," Zerin says then he points to the other boys. "These are my friends."

Zerin introduces each boy then is startled by two lower holes opening abruptly with little eyes peeking out. The creatures peering out of the lower holes seem to speak to one another in their own language. Zerin stares at the lower holes in wonder.

"What are they saying?" asks Zerin.

"They are trying to figure out your intentions. They do not know if you are good or bad," answers Nork.

"I assure you that we are good. Did we not just rescue that little creature from the trap?" asks Zerin.

"Indeed you did, but we are not used to people around

here and we are very cautious. We have had many bad experiences and wish to live separate from the rest of the world," answers Nork.

"I assure that you we mean no harm. We are simply traveling through in search of Aragopia," says Zerin.

The mention of Aragopia gets the figures looking through the smaller holes chattering to each other. Zerin takes notice. Nork speaks to the creatures in their language and they quiet down.

"I have never heard of such a place, and I know about all there is to know about in this world. There is no such place," says Nork.

"Your creatures seem to have heard of it," Zerin says then pauses and sighs. "I would think this conversation would be easier if it were face to face, rather than me talking to a hole in the wall. Will you not speak with us in a more civilized manner?" Zerin asks. "Do no fear us, we are just children and we did help the little creature."

Nork closes his eyehole followed by the two lower eye holes. Chattering in the creatures' language can be heard from the other side of the wall. Zerin looks back at the boys, his confusion shows in his face.

A moment or two goes by and Zerin's confidence wanes.

"Let's go Zerin. These creatures are strange. We are wasting our time," says Lach.

Zerin waits for a moment and notices the conversation seems to be wrapping up. Suddenly the higher eye hole opens. Zerin looks at the eye staring through.

"Though I am unsure of your intentions, Honkra-Ruku believes that we owe you for your service and we welcome you and your friends for a meal. You do look a little skinny," says Nork.

"I accept. It has been several days since we had a good meal," responds Zerin.

An invisible door toward the middle of the wooden wall slowly creaks open. It drags against dirt and leaves like an ancient entrance to long abandoned fort. Once the door is open, another small Chimihog sticks out its head. It glances at Zerin then glances at the other boys and then motions for them to follow it as it disappears back out of sight.

Zerin leads the group in. Inside isn't very different than the outside. Trees cover the grounds. The larger trees have holes at their bottoms like doorways to small huts made into the base of their trunks, forming a village. In the middle of the walled in area is a group of trees closely huddled together like a fort within a fort. At the top of that clump of trees is a tree house. As the boys enter they see many Chimihogs of all sizes staring, and more slowly exiting their hiding places to get a better view of the guests. There are big Chimihogs, medium sized Chimihogs, small Chimihogs and apparently baby Chimihogs.

A larger Chimihog walks up to Zerin.

Zerin tries to speak to the Chimihog slowly. "Where is Nork? Do you understand what I am saying, Nork?"

The Chimihog looks back at a few of the closer Chimihogs and giggles. They all giggle along. The Chimihog looks back at Zerin. "You do not have to speak so slowly. We know very well how to speak your language."

Zerin is caught off guard and a little embarrassed then says, "Then where is Nork and what is your name?

"I am Norka-Ruku. Nork is in his house. He is very

unsure of you and would like for us to get to know you first," says the Chimihog.

"Are you the leader?" asks Zerin.

Suddenly a medium sized Chimihog hurries up and bumps Norka-Ruku and stands in front. "I am the leader. My name is Honkra-Ruku," says the seemingly insulted Chimihog. "Why would you think Norka-Ruku was the leader?"

Zerin shrugs his shoulders and then says, "In many cultures the larger ones are usually the leaders."

Honkra-Ruku grunts and says, "Norka-Ruku is my wife. Are not your women bigger than you? Better for protecting you."

"Most of our women are smaller than the men," says Zerin.

Several of the medium sized Chimihogs laugh and Honkra-Ruku asks, "What good are women if they are not big enough to fight and protect you?"

Zerin and the rest of the boys are confused so Zerin changes the subject and asks, "Nork spoke of a meal. We are very hungry and would like to know when dinner will be?"

You will be eating with Nork in the upper house, but you must leave your weapons at our storage area. We cannot take any risks of assassination attempts on Nork, even if you are just children. Much evil is in the lands that surround around our humble abode.

Zerin and the boys relinquish their weapons and follow Norka-Ruku to the base of the upper house. Once at the bottom of the upper house the boys see its vast size. It is much larger close up because it extends back over more dense areas of trees.

Zerin looks up with confusion and asks, "How do we get up there?"

A voice from up high yells down. "Surely you have trees where you come from? Have you never climbed one?"

Already frustrated by having to give up his weapons, Lach is now insulted by the suggestion and responds. "We know how to climb trees. We just assumed that a man as distinguished as one who has his own house in the trees would have a more noble way of getting up to it."

"Nothing distinguished and nothing noble, I am just a regular man who lives in the woods, nothing more," answers Nork from above.

The boys, one by one, climb the interweaving trees up to the tree house. They are followed by some of the Chimihogs.

The inside of the tree house is a large open room. Large plants are scattered throughout in a pattern that separates the different areas. A large eating table sits to the side next to a kitchen area. The sleeping area is on the opposite side of the kitchen and behind the sitting area. Some chairs are dispersed throughout. A few large Chimihogs work in the kitchen preparing food.

Nork sits in a large chair in the sitting area. He looks like a regular man. He has short hair and unusual clothing as compared to most people. He looks to be about thirty years old, regular height, regular build.

"Welcome young men. Come have a seat with me so that I can learn more about you and your people," he says.

Zerin and the boys sit in a few of the chairs around this interesting stranger.

"So where do you boys come from?" asks Nork.

Lach pipes up. "We are of the Arizz people. We make our home in the Great City."

"The Great City? I do not believe I have heard of this place. Where is it?" Nork asks.

"The Great City is the center of Thrae. We the Arizz rule over all the land. The king of Thrae lives there," says Quynn.

"And we are under constant threat of those evil Trett," says Lach.

"The Trett, what are these evil creatures and who is their leader?" asks Nork.

"The Trett are evil humans, led by the most evil human, The General. They wish to take over the city and to take control of Thrae, but we will conquer them and kill all those that oppose us," says Lach.

"Humans killing humans? This does not make sense. There is so much evil in the world, how could humans fight each other?" asks Nork.

"Right now, the biggest threat in the world is The General and his Trett army. He is bent on ruling over all of Thrae," says Quynn.

"There is a much more evil threat than that one man. An evil man can be killed if he has chosen to take the dark path. Oh no, there is a much more evil power in this world and he cannot be killed. He is immortal," says Nork. "Have you not felt his wrath?"

The boys look at each other, each trying to interpret Nork's words.

"Are you talking about a Fikron?" asks Juntor.

"Fikrons are evil, but they can be killed. No, the one I speak of created the Fikron. He is much more evil than even that creature," says Nork.

"Do you speak of Alohessy?" asks Senokre.

Nork covers his ears as he speaks. "Do not even say his name. We have been free of him for a long time. I do not wish to face him again."

"We understand Alohessy to be dead," says Zerin.

"Dead?" Nork says with a shriek, "He cannot be killed. Surely someone has told you a false tale."

"It is said he was killed by Ranishi," says Senokre.

"Impossible. I have heard of Ranishi, but he is a human. No human can kill Alohessy. It was once thought the one who created Alohessy, creator of the whole world, could kill him, but little did the creator know of the menace he had brought to life. No sir, Alohessy cannot be killed. Therefore he still lives and if your people are unaware of the threat that he imposes then you should immediately go home and warn them. For if he has not attacked you yet then he lies in wait with a more sinister plan than those he had in the beginning of man," says Nork. "You must warn your people!"

"Be calm stranger, for we have heard different," says Senokre. "How do you know Alohessy is alive? Have you come across him lately?"

"It has been a long time, but I have seen the wrath of Alohessy," answers Nork.

"Our understanding is that he was killed hundreds of years ago, in the early generations of man. You say you have seen him more recently than that?" asks Zerin.

Nork stumbles for his words then responds. "Alohessy cannot be killed by a mortal. The only one capable of killing Alohessy is the god Kron and he was defeated and imprisoned by Alohessy, deep, deep in the Pryon mountains in the Caves of Talpri."

"It is told to us that Alohessy created a sword to kill the others like him, but Ranishi captured the sword and used it against him," says Senokre.

"This is interesting news to hear. But, I do not believe it. I know of the sword, but Alohessy would not leave it unguarded to be stolen by a human or any other creature. Be careful my young friends, for Alohessy is full of deceptions and will use any measure possible to destroy humans," says Nork.

Nork looks around at the Chimihogs walking here and there preparing dinner, now with nervous looks on their faces then speaks. "Enough about this evil being, dead or alive, I would not wish to be unprepared either way. But now, tell us of what you have set out to find on this grand adventure of yours."

Juntor chimes in excitedly, with a big smile on his face. "We are searching for Aragopia."

"Aragopia?" asks Nork. "I am not familiar with this place. What is it and what has it that five young boys," Nork pauses and clears his throat while giving a glance to Lach, "five young men, beg your pardon, would leave their homes and travel in foreign lands to find?"

"We are not sure that it exists," says Senokre. "In our land it is thought of as more of a myth, though there are some who say it really exists.

It is supposed to be a utopia, where there is no sickness and there is no evil. I have even heard that if an evil person enters, their hearts will suddenly soften and they will have love for all living things and cast their evil ways behind them.

I have heard that whatever lives there lives forever and they will never be hungry, because food is plenty and they will forever be happy and never long for what is outside of its borders."

"Well this is an interesting place, but I agree with your majority that this is merely a myth," answers Nork. "Who or what would be so powerful that they could create such a place. Alohessy perhaps, but he is far too evil to create a land of peace and good."

"It was created by Brigal," says Juntor, jumping back into the conversation.

"Brigal?" asks Nork, taken aback. "Brigal is a cowardly pawn of Alohessy. Perhaps Brigal is powerful enough to create such a place, but for peaceful purposes, I think not. Brigal works for Alohessy."

"It is said that Alohessy left Brigal to fight the human armies, but the humans defeated Brigal and out of fear, Brigal went into exile to hide from Alohessy and he saw the error of his ways, therefore creating Aragopia," says Senokre.

"This is all very interesting and hopeful, but I fear that if there is this Aragopia, it is another trick of Alohessy. I would wish for you to venture somewhere else. I believe you may be walking into a trap at this place," says Nork.

"How do you know so much about the history of this world?" asks Lach. "You have the appearance of being maybe thirty years old at the most, yet you speak as if you have experienced things that happened hundreds of years ago."

"My appearance may deceive and I may be older than I look, but around here, letting more information about yourself get out is a guarantee for some trouble from anyone who may seek such information, for there is no one who would search for me unless their intentions were bad," says Nork. "But I will tell this. I know more about the beginnings of this world than any living man."

"Perhaps you know where Aragopia is and have lived there so that you may be older than you appear and now you will try to turn us away, so that you can keep this place all to yourself?" asks Lach defiantly.

Zerin looks at Lach and says. "Be calm with you words Lach. We are guests in this man's house and he offers us food. He may not be telling us all that he knows, but I do not think he has any bad intentions."

"Nork looks at Lach for a moment and says. "A lot of anger I see in you. I never perceived a human to have that hint of evil in him, but now maybe I see. Be not insulted by my words, because what I mean by evil is not an intention to do evil, but a fire inside a person that, if not controlled, can turn good intentions into evil deeds. This now I see as why even humans, as good of a creature as they are can still stray onto the wrong path."

Lach stares at Nork for a moment with ill intentions, but his words break Lach's mental stance and forces him to break the lock between his eyes and the wise man's. He looks down at the floor.

"This is disappointing news, indeed. I have been hiding here so long that I have missed the many changes that have taken place in this world. I would hope that someday that man, at least most, would learn to get along and to know that there are far greater evils in this world than your neighbor. If you fight with your neighbor, who will be watching your homes for intruders with far worse intentions than a squabble with a friend?" asks Nork.

A large Chimihog walks over to Nork and the boys and in a very soft and articulate voice says, "The food is prepared. Would you like to come to the table and have your meal?"

"Good debate makes my stomach long for food. Let us fill ourselves so that we may energize our minds for the next round," says Nork.

The boys nod and get up and follow Nork to the large table in the eating area. Nork sits at the head and the boys take seats here and there. They are joined by a few Chimihogs, including Honkra-Ruku and Norka-Ruku.

Several Chimihogs bring food to the table and help the boys prepare their plates. The food is plenty with a large fowl cooked and steaming vegetables sitting in the middle of the table. There are potatoes and corn and butter. The boys look around in wonder. They have never seen so much food at one setting and some of the food they had never seen or heard of. They eat the food they are familiar with and test, sometimes reluctantly, foods that are new to them. Some they like and some they do not, but this feast will leave no full grown man hungry, so definitely it fills the bellies of these five young men.

As the meal comes to an end, each diner sits back in their seats with full stomachs. Nork initiates the conversation. "Tell me some of your journey so far. What have you seen? Have you encountered any challenges or evil creatures along the way?"

The boys tell a little of the small tribe of people that wanted to eat Juntor, at which the Chimihogs are grossed out by and Nork is so amazed it overshadows his disgust at the possibility of one human eating another.

The boys tell of the giraffes that they had seen, which to Nork and the Chimihogs was not an unusual sight, for often they would see a Giraffe peek its long neck over their walls, sometimes to eat leaves from a tree that was inside the fort and sometimes just to get a peek at the unusual creature that is a Chimihog.

The conversation slowly works its way back to the subject of Aragopia, to which Nork is still very skeptical.

"You may stay here as long as you want. When you do leave, I hope that you will not pursue this Aragopia. I believe Alohessy is behind it, but you all seem to be strong willed and determined and I will not pretend that I could make you do or not do whatever it is you have already set your mind to," says Nork.

"We have come too far on this journey to just now stop and turn back. That would be like failure and we don't intend on going back to our homes as cowards," says Lach.

Nork nods his head and ponders for a moment. Nork signals for a Chimihog who comes over to him and whispers in its ear and the Chimihog hurries out of the tree house.

Nork looks at the boys again and says, "You have set out on an adventure and you wish to have a sense of accomplishment before you go back to your homes. What if I give you a task that neither I nor the Chimihogs are brave enough to tackle, though it is of serious importance? Would you be willing to change your goals and at the same time repay the Chimihogs for this glorious meal they have prepared for us? If it is danger you seek, there may be. If it is new lands you seek, then you may find them. Would you be interested?"

The boys look around at each other for a moment and then Quynn speaks up. "We would be willing to pay you back for this meal, but as far as this mission, we would need to know more."

As Quynn finishes speaking two Chimihogs enter the tree house, one large one called Gorka-tuku and one medium sized, called Brilka-tuku. They have sorrow and concern on their faces and Nork signals for them to come and stand beside him.

"This is Gorka-tuku and Brilka-tuku. Their son Brenka-uku has been missing for about a month now and we are all very concerned," says Nork.

"Have you searched for him?" asks Lach.

"Oh no, there is far too much danger for us to leave these walls," says Gorka-tuku.

"But your child is missing. Why would you not search for him?" asks Lach.

"We did search for him, but he apparently has gone beyond our walls," says Brilka-tuku.

The frustration grows on Lach's face as he can't understand why these Chimihogs refuse to leave the city walls to search for their child. Nork notices this and jumps in to explain to the boys, more about the Chimihogs.

"We are very scared of what lies outside of these walls," he says. "We do not seek adventure, because it includes danger and we just want to live without trouble. Little Brenka-uku decided to journey outside our walls. For what reason we do not know, but now he is missing and we can only hope that no great harm has come to him. We would like to search for him, but if he hasn't come back, then whoever we send to search for him may not come back either.

That is a risk we do not wish to take. We have not the abilities to fight any evil attackers, especially that evil Alohessy. We are only safe inside our walls and can only hope for Brenka-uku's safe return, whether by his efforts or by someone who is brave and willing to find him."

"So this is your request? You would like for us to find this Brenka-uku and bring him back here safely?" asks Lach.

"It would be a noble deed and much more satisfying than finding the mythical land you search for," answers Nork.

"I would very much like to find Aragopia or at least find out whether it truly exists or not, for there are so many tales about it, most of which are very hard to believe," says Senokre. "So as the instigator of this search for Aragopia, I would be willing to concede to your request if my friends would be willing to go with me."

"I will go. I see the good in these Chimihogs and also their fear of the outside world. I would not want to be in this situation and I would gladly take help if I were, so I will go with you, Senokre," Zerin says.

On cue, Juntor speaks up. "I will go also."

Lach and Quynn do not respond immediately. Lach has most of his goal set on running across a Fikron for he would like to kill this most evil creature. Quynn's reluctance is something deeper, but as it is hard to read his emotions, no one knows the source of his pause.

"I will go," Lach says as he finally agrees, realizing that there may be some evil behind the fact that the young Chimihog never returned.

Quynn looks around at his friends and being aware that he has been outvoted and due to the fact that he would not attempt to find Aragopia on his own, finally agrees as well.

"We will be most grateful," says Brilka-tuku.

"It is settled then. You shall set out in search of little Brenka-uku," says Nork. "But first you should get some rest. You may stay here as long as you need to gather your strength so that you may be hearty for your mission. We will set you up some beds here in the tree house so that you may rest at least for tonight. Do you know when you think you would be ready to search for Brenka-uku?

"I believe a good night's rest will be enough. We shall set out in the morning when we wake," says Zerin.

The other boys agree.

So the boys have a little more conversation with Nork while their beds are made ready. Juntor is the first to jump into a bed and go to sleep. Slowly one by one the boys exit the fellowship and climb into their beds and fall asleep. Nork watches the sleeping boys for a little while, all along thinking with admiration.

"You will all be heroes one day. I can foresee it. I do not know when or what the conflict, but one day you will all be hailed as saviors of this planet," Nork whispers to himself before getting up, and as he walks away he says, "They truly are an amazing people, these humans, the greatest creation." Nork disappears into his sleeping area.

Chapter 6

The morning sun peeks through the windows of the tree house. The songs of many birds enter from outside. Inside the tree house is somber. The boys sleep, except for Zerin, who quietly sits in a chair pondering a game plan to rescue the missing Chimihog. He felt a strong bond with the little Chimihog that he saved from the pit and now feels a strong drive to safely rescue Brenka-uku and return him to his people.

Lach is the next to wake and the other three, one by one, arise. A few Chimihogs have come to the tree house and fixed a breakfast for the boys, so the boys have a quick bite and then pack up the supplies given to them by their host for the journey. Zerin looks around for Nork, but Nork is nowhere to be found. When the boys are ready, they say goodbye to the Chimihogs and leave the tree house.

At the gate, as they are walking out, Zerin turns to the Chimihogs, who now watch in a large group. "I will do everything in my power to return Brenka-uku to your tribe and to his family. You have my word," he says as he bows then turns to follow the rest of the boys out.

The next leg of the adventure takes the boys on through forest. They continue to revel at all the sights and sounds that make up the wood land. Rare large trees stand as guardians with outstretched arms, with many hands of leaves over the path of dead brush and straw that the boys travel, still heading toward the ever growing white tops of the Pryon Mountains. The peaks are shaped like large jagged teeth rising into a sea of blue, surrounded by lumps of cotton that seem to pass by and through like ghosts journeying on a mission of their own. Occasionally a bird of some sort flies past the high peaks of the mountains, riding the wind like a surfer on an invisible wave.

Juntor spots a small pack of wild, little dog-like creatures, which cower behind a bush at the site of the group of boys passing though their lands. He points them out to the other boys as they pass.

"I would like to try to catch one of them for a pet," says Juntor.

"They may be small, but they are wild and would probably maul all of us pretty easily if we were to try to catch one. You should stick with the animals we are familiar with in our lands for catching and making pets," Quynn says.

"Very well, but at least we could give them a name

since we may be the first humans to ever see this type of dog," Juntor suggests.

"I would find it hard to believe no human has ever seen one of these types of dogs, but why not. What shall we call them then?" Quynn asks, now liking the idea.

"I do not know. I will have to think a bit," answers Juntor.

The boys continue on, all along throwing out names for the creatures. They turn their noses up at some names and they take into consideration others. It becomes a bit of a game that helps pass the time as they continue to travel.

As the day nears evening, the boys come to see an opening out of the forest ahead. It is the end of the tree line and appears to be a clear trek to the base of the mountains. The boys hurry along in an effort to beat the dark to the end of the trees in order to evaluate the terrain for tomorrow's journey. As the base of the mountain gets closer it takes the appearance of a wall with small, black windows dotted all about.

As the boys get closer they find a surprise, for being aware of a place called the Caves of Talpri, they did not know that the caves were set inside a canyon. They reach the edge of the woods and find out the forest has ended because the land has ended, or so it would seem, because between the edge of the forest and the caves is a huge ravine, splitting the land, like an ancient river had washed all the soil between away, for about a mile or two. On the other side, the walls have streaks running back and forth between the cave openings, like a marker had drawn zigzag patterns connecting the black dots across a rock canvas.

The boys walk to the very edge of the canyon and look

down. No such luck as trails and paths to the bottom on this side as there is only a sheer drop off of a hundred feet or more to the bottom.

They look at each other, disappointed. They look to the west and see the gorge go on as far as they can see. They look to the east and see, in the distance, that the ravine begins to become shallow, till the two sides meet again, like an arrow pointing the boys in the direction they should choose.

"It is getting dark. We should set up camp now, so that we may have some time to sit and discuss tomorrow's plans. I do not get a good feeling about going east, though we have no other choice. We will be getting very close to the Trett's roaming areas, so it would seem the most dangerous part of our journey so far, will be tomorrow," says Quynn.

The boys agree and set up camp. Quieter they are now, feeling the truth in Quynn's words, but ever resilient all the more. Once camp is established, they sit around a small fire and discuss their plans until it is time to sleep.

The sun rises in the east, shining on the right side of the mountains, creating a split between light and dark as the eastward facing slope delays the sun's gleam from reaching all things west of the towering peak. The eastern sky is orange, like fire upon the land that awaits the boys. The further east they go, the closer to the danger they will be.

The boys stand together, all of their things packed and ready to go. They have been up since the sun first peeked over the horizon in the east, but uncertainty has delayed their departure, though they now are building up a last bit of confidence before they move on. Finally they set out on the next leg of their journey.

The sun continues to rise and the day comes to full light, showing the magnificence of the rising mountains, now to the left of the boys with the opposing cliff face and all the openings to the labyrinth of caves. Lach thinks he spies a black creature moving at the bottom of the ravine, but loses sight of it and is forced to give up looking for it. The forest to their right finally begins to give way to more open land. This concerns them a little, because they had become used to having the trees for cover, but they continue on. The opening to ravine gets closer and closer as the cave openings are now further behind.

Just before the opening to the ravine is a patch of trees. The boys decide to take a rest there. It is a good spot to get out of the open and to get some shade and relief from the sun hanging high above. The wind blows, creating a nice cool breeze through the trees, rustling the leaves creating a serenading sound that causes some of the boys to become groggy. Juntor gives in and lays his head against the trunk of the tree he sits beside and nods off. The cool air on their face brings relief from the rigorous and hot march toward the ravine opening. They enjoy the scenic view of the canyon and mountains.

After a little while the wind dies down and the noise through the tree subsides, but not to silence for another sound crawls over the near horizon and weaves through the small patch of trees to the boys, where they relax. The sound is of men, but not of just men of a nearby tribe, but noises made be fighting men, warriors, apparently in a nearby camp. The question though is which warriors, Trett or Arizz? The beating of drums and the shouting of commands that would come from a training exercise grow louder and louder as the wind continues to withdraw its song.

Lach is the first to hear it, being always in a warrior mindset. One by one, the boys become aware as well, except for Juntor who sleeps. His sleep is interrupted as Lach throws a small stick at him to get his attention. The boys peek around the bunch of trees that now serve as their hiding place.

They are silent as they evaluate the noises. Senokre is the first to break the silence and he asks, "Who do you think they are?"

"It is hard to tell if they are friend or foe. The Arizz and the Trett have very similar command patterns. I do not know," says Quynn.

"I do not know either, but it would be better for us to assume they are the enemy, until we see otherwise," suggests Zerin.

"The opening to the ravine is just over there. Can we make it there without being detected?" asks Senokre.

"I do not want to get trapped in that ravine with an army of Trett after us. There would be no escape," Quynn warns.

"I can see the opening of the ravine, but I cannot see the camp of men. Surely we can make it to the opening before they see us," says Senokre.

"One thing we will have to be concerned about is scouts," says Lach. "They probably have scouts or lookouts away from the camp. That is who we would need to be wary of seeing us."

"Then we should send out a scout ourselves," says Zerin, "someone to find out exactly who they are and where they are."

"I agree. I will go," says Lach.

"Senokre is the most trained in the area of stealth and tracking.   Perhaps he should be the one who goes," Zerin says cautiously, knowing that Lach will be offended.

"I just volunteered to go and you just overlook me?" Lach asks as he and Zerin lock eyes.

"I agree with Zerin, Lach. It is not that we overlook you, but we know, as well as you, that if you come across any Trett, that you would rather fight them than avoid them. Since our mission is not to battle an army of Trett warriors, I believe Senokre is the better person for the job and as the oldest of our group I am taking a firm stand on this decision," says Quynn, showing the leadership skills that the elders of the military academy have foreseen.

Lach stands for a moment, offended and angry. He takes a deep breath and throws his hands up in disgust then walks away to the edge of the ravine and stands.

Quynn looks at Zerin and they exchange a moment of relief, knowing they may have dodged a bullet known as Lach then Quynn speaks up. "OK Senokre, be cautious of their scouts and search out this camp. We will wait here for you."

Senokre nods and prepares himself then, with stealth, he sneaks toward the source of the noise.

While they wait, Zerin walks over to his friend who still stands at the edge of the ravine, looking out into the vast opening in the land. He stands beside Lach and joins him in viewing the landscape and says, "Do not be insulted, my friend. We are all very capable warriors. But, we also have specialized skills and while no one doubts your abilities, you must not forget that this is a team and we all need to be involved."

"I just fear other people's mistakes. If I can do it

myself, then I can be more certain of the outcome," says Lach.

"No matter how great a warrior, not all things can be done by one man alone. In war it takes a team of people to get a job done. This I learned from Olkar. Surely he has taught you the same lesson?"

"He has, but I look at our king and he is no leader. Every day it seems The General moves closer and closer to victory. Our military leaders are not strong enough to conquer him and I fear that I may not reach the age when I may join in the fight, before the Arizz leadership's mistakes finally allow the Trett to take over. Then what do I do? Then I would have to be a part of a rebel army of Arizz, still led by the same leaders who lost the kingdom in the first place. They would fear my abilities and I would have to wrestle power from them, before I could even begin to fight The General," says Lach, showing that he has thought long and hard over these possibilities for some time now.

"You are trying to see the future. I do agree with being prepared for anything, but to predict the future, as you are trying to, would bring unnecessary stress. We cannot control our ages. We can only continue to prepare for the future, no matter what circumstances arrive, and deal with them as they come along," says Zerin.

Lach nods his head. He stands silent, still in deep thought as Zerin walks away.

About an hour goes by. The boys sit amongst the trees, each in their own train of thought. Approaching footsteps bring them out of their daze. It is Senokre, who breathes heavy and has excitement in his eyes. The boys stand with anticipation for information on their faces.

"There is a Trett army about a half a mile past the opening to the ravine. The terrain has a few trees and some hills, so they will not be able to see us. I did see two scouts out roaming around, but they were heading away from the ravine. I believe if we go right now, we can get into the ravine and out of danger," Senokre tells the boys.

So the boys gather their things and begin to work their way to the opening of the ravine which sits just a few hundred feet away. As they walk, they carefully scan the area for any other scouts or surprises that may lurk. They safely arrive at the opening.

It is very rocky, but gently slopes down into the deeper land. As the ravine widens, the slope widens going deeper and deeper into the ravine. The sun is still high in the sky, so there is no limitation on the light that is allowed to enter the low lying terrain. At the bottom of the slope the land flattens back out. There is a wash curving back and forth through the ravine, a remnant of a dried up river or maybe a seasonal river.

The threat of being seen by anyone at the top of the ravine diminishes now as the boys reach the bottom. Small bushes dot the grounds and the boys stay close to them when they can. The look of caution on the boys' faces slowly relaxes as the threat of being spotted dwindles. But, just as the boys think they are out of danger a noise from the south side of the ravine catches their attentions. The sound of rocks falling reveals a man, a Trett scout attempting to scurry up the side undetected.

"It's a scout!" yells Lach. We have to stop him before he tells the other Trett."

Lach takes off after the scout. The scout stumbles on a loose rock and tumbles down the side of the ravine to the bottom. The boys follow Lach. Lach arrives to the scout as the scout is regaining his composure. He sees the boy coming toward him with his sword drawn and draws his own sword. The two battle ready warriors face off. The other boys arrive and draw their swords.

"Stand down Trett warrior, or I shall strike you down," says Lach.

The scout looks over the boys and notices that they are Arizz and says, "A bit far from your homes aren't you, little Arizz boys?"

"Not as far away from home as you are about to feel, if you do not relinquish your weapons," says Lach.

The scout laughs and says, "Mouthy little boy, you do not wish to have your lesson today from me, for I will cut out your tongue, and you can mumble your impotent threats from now on."

Zerin steps forward to intervene and hopefully delay Lach's attack. "You are outnumbered. You must surrender."

"I have defeated full grown men, twice your size and of the same number as you. Why should I surrender to less of a threat?" asks the scout.

The scout doesn't give Zerin a chance to answer and unknown to the boys has some dirt in his hand and throws it into Lach's eyes and then swipes his sword at Zerin. Zerin loses his balance as he dodges and slips on the loose rocks. Quynn steps forward and exchanges swordplay for a moment until Senokre enters the battle. The scout is a good fighter and causes Senokre and Quynn to get in each other's way, hindering their efforts. A kick to the stomach knocks Quynn out of the battle.

Lach attacks the scout, now having just gotten the dirt out of his eyes, but still blinking heavily. Senokre backs away from the fight. The scout gets the better of Lach, because Lach is still partially blinded. The scout knocks Lach's sword out of his hand. Lach dives for the sword and the scout attempts to stab him, but Zerin runs into the scout, knocking him to the ground.

The scout regains his composure and looks to see now, Zerin and Lach standing side by side, swords drawn, ready for battle.

"Let's hope you two work better as a team than did your friends," says the scout as he attacks.

Senokre, Juntor and Quynn watch the battle and see what they know already. Lach and Zerin move in perfect unity. For every strike, a defense back to a strike to a defense in perfect harmony. It only takes a few minutes and the cocky scout is overwhelmed and he surrenders his sword and begs for mercy. Lach prepares for the fatal blow, his sword held high over his head.

"No, Lach! He has surrendered," says Zerin.

Lach lowers his sword and backs away, still emotional, his mind still set in battle mode.

"What shall we do with him?" asks Quynn.

"We must take him prisoner until we are far enough away from the Trett army," says Zerin.

"Then what, let him go?" asks Lach. "So then I can look over my shoulder for the rest of our journey?"

Senokre looks at the fear and surprise on the scout's face and says. "I do not believe he will be a threat any longer. He has been broken, defeated by two boys. Tie him up, we must get moving. We haven't much daylight left."

The shadows begin to creep in as the sun sets down the ravine. The boys have traveled within sight of the first cave opening, but to be safe, they choose to set up camp at what they hope is a safe distance, to avoid any surprises during the night. They tie the scout to a small lonely tree that stands by the wash, as if it is waiting for its next drink. Each boy will take a turn to keep watch and to keep an eye on the scout. Senokre is the first to take watch and the other boys settle down and fall fast asleep.

It is late into the night, the stars shine brightly over the ravine. The moon peeks out from behind the towering Pryon Mountains standing above the canyon. Juntor has been on watch now for a little while, and grows bored of watching the scout sleep as he sits tied against the tree. Juntor fights back his sleepy eyelids. The battle goes back and forth, each time it seems he will lose, he manages to force his eyes open again and readjust his body to continue to maintain guard.

As Juntor begins to enter another tug of war with his eyelids, they begin to close, but only for a split second. As the lids fall, he sees the image of the man asleep against the tree. Juntor's eyes see black for a moment as his sleep makes a hard push for victory then Juntor forces his eyes back open and is startled to see the scene that lay in front of him now. Where there was once a man tied to a tree, now just a torn rope, half wrapped around the tree.

Juntor sits up, rubs his eyes and looks around. There is no sign of the scout. "How did he escape so fast?" Juntor asks himself, now feeling the fear of being looked down upon by his friends for not doing his job.

Juntor wakes Zerin to tell him of what has happened. He walks with Juntor to the tree and examines the evidence.

"He was here and I just blinked my eyes and then he was gone," says Juntor.

Zerin looks over the ropes. They seem to have been torn, not cut by a sharp blade. Zerin awakens the rest of the boys. They all stand around the tree trying to figure out this mystery.

After a while Quynn says. "It is just too dark to figure out what happened here. I can't see another Trett warrior freeing him and not attacking us while we slept."

"Well we surely cannot sleep safely now. It appears that this will become a long night, because we all will have to stand guard now and be ready for anything, until morning when we can better know what is going on," says Lach.

So the boys sit in a circle back to back, their swords in their hands. The darkness only magnifies their concerns, and all they can do is wait. Wait for morning light or wait for an attack, an attack from what, they are not eager to find out. Sleep will be no challenge when fear joins in the struggle to stay awake.

Chapter 7

The morning light comes not soon enough for the boys as the view of the tree and scene of the disappearance becomes clear. Lach is the first to approach the tree and he looks around for evidence. The other boys join him, all looking around for clues.

Lach holds the torn rope while pointing at a long scratch in the tree and says, "This does not look like any cut of a sword or knife."

"I do not see any sign of footprints of a man or men," says Senokre.

"Why did you fall asleep Juntor? You are aware of our situation and know it was very important to have no more surprises than we are already in for," says Quynn.

"I did not fall asleep. I admit I was tired, but I only blinked and what was there a split second before, was gone," Juntor says, ready to defend himself.

"You had to have fallen asleep. There is no way that he could have escaped so fast. He would have to cut the ropes, remove them and walk away without leaving any tracks. That would take time," says Lach.

Zerin comes to Juntor's defense, knowing that Juntor being the youngest made him an easy target. "I believe Juntor is telling the truth. I do not believe he would make such a mistake knowing the peril that it could put us in."

"Maybe you thought you only blinked, but actually fell asleep, not knowing that fact when you awoke," suggests Lach.

"No! I did not fall asleep, I did not dream. I even looked at the moon and it had not moved. I did not fall asleep. Whatever happened literally happened in a blink of an eye," Juntor responds with conviction.

All eyes are on Juntor as he defends himself and Lach counters his statements and asks, "What can accomplish this feat in a blink of an eye?"

"I have had all night to ponder the possibilities and the conclusion I have come up with is the only one that would make since. I recall Senokre's words about the description Hedgeparth had made about a creature so black and cunning that it could be right beside you in a full moon and you would not be aware until its claws ripped into your flesh," Juntor states as Senokre gets a look of awareness on his face and turns back to look upon the ground around the tree. Juntor finishes his words saying, "I believe a Fikron may have taken him."

"A Fikron!" exclaims Quynn. "You have thought long and hard about this, but it seems for an excuse rather than a legitimate reason."

Senokre speaks from beside the tree as he kneels down at a marking in the dirt and interjects, "I thought I saw this strange track in the ground, but I did not consider what it was until Juntor brought it to our attention. Hedgeparth had described the Fikron that he encountered as being cat-like. This is a footprint, very similar to a cat, a very large cat, and now I can see the marking of what must be its claws."

He stands and says, "I agree with Juntor. I believe a Fikron came in the night and took the poor scout while we slept, and in the blink of an eye, for Juntor did not fail us."

Lach and Quynn go over to look over the print.

"There is no blood though," Lach says.

"All the more gruesome for the Trett warrior," says Quynn, now believing Juntor. "I am an enemy of the Trett, but I feel sorry for the scout, because he has been taken alive to meet his fate later, at the hands of an evil animal. I do not wish that horror on any man."

"Then we are now in grave danger and must approach the rest of this journey as such. Apparently we are in the realm where Fikrons roam and one man will not be enough to satisfy them for long. From here on out we must be on top of our game. Nork said we may find danger if we wanted it. I believe we have," says Zerin.

"Let us continue our mission then, but always have you swords at the ready. Most likely these Fikron's live in these caves we are about to explore and once we enter, we will have no place to run. We will have to fight," says Quynn.

"I look forward to it," says Lach, having been relatively bored so far on this adventure, now excited about the prospect of a battle with a Fikron or Fikrons.

The boys pack their things in a hurry and make their way to the first cave opening, hoping that the Chimihog had similar intentions.

The opening of the first cave is about two paths up from the base of the ravine, about twenty feet up. The path leading to the opening is one zig and one zag. It is very thin and unstable as if it is used by creatures that are very familiar with walking alongside steep slopes. The boys make it up to the opening which is about eight feet high and ten feet wide. The floor shows years and years of use with many footprints roughing up the ground making it impossible to distinguish one print from another. Looking from the outside, the light allows for a view of several feet into the cave until the shadow marks the beginning of a long darkness.

The boys pause at the opening and take a deep breath. All their claimed bravery will now be put to the test, far beyond any tests so far. After a moment and a few exchanges of glances they all nod, take a deep breath and begin the underground stage of their journey.

After being in the cave for a while, the boys are surprised at how much their eyes have adapted to the darkness. They can make out the images of each other and can see enough not to run into any walls. They are a little uncomfortable with all the rubbish of varying sizes that their feet kick or crush and sometimes stumble over. It is too dark to determine what the makeup is of the items on the floor, but in the dark, boys' imaginations can get away from them and thoughts of bones and skulls and creepy creatures that crawl on the ground run through their minds. The worst part is the occasional crunching sounds when they step on some of these invisible objects, but cautiously they push on, deeper and deeper into the underground labyrinth. A smell grows as well, the further in they travel.

"Is it just me or has anyone noticed that smell, which gets worse the deeper in we get. What kind of rotting carcasses lie in these caves? I am ready to gag at any moment," says Lach, clearly annoyed by the disturbance.

It is a bad smell, but as our eyes have adapted to the darkness of this cave, so should our noses become adapted to the bizarre stench," says Zerin.

The boys reach a fork in the tunnels. One way seems to be a continuation of the cave they are already in and the other one juts to the right and is much smaller. The boys pause to ponder which opening to take.

"I do not like this cave as it is, even though it is broad and not smothering, so I definitely do not wish to enter a smaller hole," says Quynn.

The boys do not argue, all carrying the same consensus, so they follow the path into the larger opening which begins to slope slightly upwards further in, until a few tiny rays of light can be seen coming from the ceiling.

"We must be close to the top of the canyon. The light comes in and we can see a little better now," says Senokre.

The boys pause to evaluate their environment a little more thorough, now that they can see well. The cave appears to decrease in size up a ways and there is another opening on the right, just before. The light also reveals what lies on the ground of the cave. Remnants of many things, due to years and years of use, decorate the floor. There are some bones, mostly of small animals. There are the shells of bugs, long since deceased and some perhaps from shedding. There are some live bugs, beetle like, and some centipede types as well. There are also brittle rocks that do not seem to belong to the terrain of the caves, perhaps washed in by some flood or giant river flowing through the canyon, many years ago.

As the boys observe the terrain and consider their next move, a noise races through the cave to their ears, startling them out of their thought.

"What was that?" asks Juntor first, his eyes wide.

"I do not know, but it sounded like something yelling," says Zerin.

"Maybe it is someone in trouble, because it sounded like a sound a man would make and not an animal," says Lach.

"It did sound like a man, but it sounded more like a yell of anger and frustration than that of fear or anguish," says Senokre.

Again the noise, the same as before, races through the tunnel. They stay very quiet and try to catch more of the sound. Again the noise floats its way through the cave.

"It sounds like it is coming from that smaller opening ahead. I am not eager to find out what it is, but we are on a mission to find the missing Chimihog, and though I have heard one talk, I have not heard one yell. I do not know if that is the source of the noise, but I believe we should investigate," says Quynn.

"I agree. We should go and see, but have your swords at the ready for we do not know what, if any, danger this entails. As we do not know what the yell of a Chimihog sounds like, nor do we know what the yell of a Fikron is either," says Lach with his sword already drawn.

The boys walk to the opening, where the noise seems to exit, with their swords held at the ready. They gather around the opening and Lach slowly peeks his head in then pulls it back out and says, "This tunnel goes about a hundred feet and then, at its end off to the right, I see light peeking out, as if there is some sort of room or opening to the outside world."

The boys enter the tunnel one by one. It is only big enough for them to walk single file, though. As they close in on the lit area, they hear more clearly the noises that originate from there.

"You are not friendly. You have to be friendly! This is a fun game, why don't you play? Argh, I hate you," says a sluggish voice from the lighted room.

The boys slowly creep closer and closer to the lit opening. Noises of things falling and being thrown clang through the tunnel and on past the boys.

"Play, play with me!" says the voice, seemingly disappointed with whatever circumstances it is in. "I feed you and give you things and take good care of you, but you do not return my favor, bad little Fuzzy, bad!"

"I don't know what that's about," comments Quynn, who shares the same sentiment as the boys; that of not having a clue what this seemingly nutty character is talking about.

Lach arrives at the entrance first and peeks in while the other boys wait anxiously behind him for an answer to this new and very weird mystery.

It is a room made from a large opening in rock. There is a makeshift bed lying on the floor against the wall on the right side. There is a black fire pit for cooking on the opposite side of the room. Above it are vegetables and plants dangling by a rope from the ceiling. There are items such as ragged clothing and some worn out tools, like things stolen from outsiders, whenever the creature that lives here would venture out of darkness of these caves.

A noise comes from another opening that is toward the back of the makeshift living quarters. Lach continues to peer in and draws back a little when he sees the noise maker enter from a back room. It is an ugly creature, very manlike, but one that would not be accepted by normal people. It has a hunched back that is covered by a ragged shirt that doesn't cover a flabby belly which hangs over a ragged loin cloth that hangs down to knobby knees on toothpick sized legs that have many scars on them. Its arms are of two different lengths, one being thinner and less mobile than the other arm which looks normal. Its face is no less stomach wrenching. Its eyes are of two different sizes and not symmetric, as one seems a little lower than the other. The lower eye squints and seems to not work in sequence with the other eye when the creature looks around. It has a short flat nose with some crusted up, tan colored substance on its upper lip as if the substance had come from its nose and dried. Its mouth slants slightly and the creature seems to breathe through one side more than the other. When it talks, as it continues complaining, the inside of its mouth show many missing teeth. The few teeth that remain are long and some are jagged, like they have not yet completed the rotting process and are soon to make their exit as well.

As Lach stares at the bizarre man, deep in focus in order to take in all the strangeness of this man's appearance, he is caught by surprise by the stench that has snuck upon his nose.

Not slight like the smell was before in which Lach has grown somewhat accustomed, but now full on, like the smell of old rotting vegetables mixed with body odor and rotten eggs. Lach almost loses his balance as his nose becomes aware of this pungent attack and blinks his eyes as they begin to burn. Although the man stands on the far end of the room on the opposite side of Lach's position, the smell travels as if the smelly thing was right next to him.

Lach leans back covering his nose and sees the boys standing there, already holding their noses.

"What is it?" asks Zerin in a whisper.

Lach shakes his head and notions for Zerin, who is next in line to take a look. Zerin slips around Lach and looks in. After a moment of amazed observance, Lach signals for the boys to back out to the larger cave.

The boys emerge from the tunnel one by one and gather in a circle and Quynn asks, "What did you see and what caused that awful smell?"

Lach and Zerin describe what they had seen then Zerin suggests, "We need to find out what it is yelling at. It called something Fuzzy and the Chimihogs are fuzzy creatures. Maybe Brenka-uku is in there with him."

"How can he stand that smell and why would he want to live with such a foul thing as what you have described?" asks Quynn.

"Maybe the Chimihog is not there voluntarily. Maybe he is being held prisoner," suggests Senokre.

"Its words did not sound like a captor speaking to his prisoner," Lach says, still a little perplexed by what he had seen.

"Well, we have been sent on this mission to find the Chimihog. So if he is in danger then we need to rescue him and if he is here by his own choice, then surely this strange man is of no threat to us and would allow us to simply have a few words with Brenka-uku and be on our way," says Zerin.

"I believe his smell alone is dangerous enough," says Lach, who is very annoyed by the horrific smell that still haunts his nose.

"Nevertheless, we must honor our word," says Zerin. "So who will go and speak with him?"

No one volunteers so the boys decide to go together and brave the pungent aroma that permeates through the tunnel. Somehow, probably by the design of the older boys, Juntor is first in line and the first who will have to enter the room.

Juntor peeks in.

"There is no one here," he says.

"All the boys file into the smelly room and look around.

"Maybe he is in the other room again," says Lach.

The boys cautiously approach the opening on the back side of the room. There is another opening on one side of the small rock room, leading to yet another shadowy cave. On the other side sits a cage like structure. Inside the cage is a furry creature, sitting in a dark corner of the makeshift prison.

"Is that him?" asks Juntor.

"Brenka-uku, are you Brenka-uku?" Quynn asks the caged creature.

The furry animal looks up at the boys then reveals himself from out of the shadow. It is a Chimihog and he identifies himself as Brenka-uku.

"Where is that creature that has locked you up?" asks Zerin.

"He has gone to gather. I do not know how long he will be gone. Sometimes he stays gone for days and sometimes he is only gone for a few minutes," says Brenka-uku.

"We will hurry to free you then. I do not wish to ever see that creature again," says Zerin.

The boys work to open the cage while explaining to Brenka-uku who they are and their meeting with the Chimihogs. Finally they open the cage door and they all hurry back out to the wider cave. They take a moment to catch their breath then head toward the cave's exit.

They see the light increase as they close in on the exit to the outside world, but a shadow and a snarl stop them in their tracks. The boys see at the opening, a black figure walking on all fours about to enter.

"It is a Fikron," whispers Brenka-uku.

Lucky for the boys, the shadow of the cave keeps their presence unknown to the Fikron and they are able to sneak back deeper into the cave.

"What do we do?" asks Quynn.

"Let us kill it," says Lach.

"We are at a disadvantage in the close confines of this cave. It would be a bad choice to fight in this situation," says Quynn

"We must go back to where we came from or at least close enough to where the smell is strong. Fikrons do not like that smell and will avoid any area that has it," says Brenka-uku

So the boys hurry back toward the smelly creature's den. The smell's intensity slowly increases till Lach stops the group and says, "This is far enough. I cannot take any more of that odor."

The boys stand quietly, listening for any sounds that would signify the approach of the Fikron.

After a few tense moments, Lach, who struggles most with the smell, says," I would fight any man or creature, but I do not believe I could fight this stinking thing. The smell would be too much for my senses to take and I would not be able to fight at my best."

He looks at Brenka-uku and asks, "What is that creature called?

"He calls himself Wilber," answers Brenka-uku.

Lach shakes his head, but being aware of his revelation of not being able to fight, creates a new problem as the boys hear approaching, the sluggish speech of Wilber who is panicking. He apparently has just learned that his prisoner has escaped and is now desperately searching for him.

"Why did he take you prisoner anyway?" asks Juntor, as the other boys try to decide what to do.

"He said he wanted me to be his friend," Brenka-uku says as he shrugs his shoulders.

"This way," Quynn interrupts, leading the boys to the smaller cave they passed earlier in their cave adventure. "We now have two enemies to avoid."

The light that was so helpful in the other part of the cave gives way to the darkness that controls most of this underground maze. The boys hurry as fast as possible, occasionally bumping into walls and sudden turns in their path. They pass several turn offs, not having the time to stop and decide if they would be a better route. Wilber is hot on their trail. The darkness in this area is the blackest they have encountered and they begin to run into each other, which leads to the next misfortune.

Quynn, who is leading the party, stops suddenly, but before he is able to let the other boys know, Lach, who is next in line runs into him. A yell that quickly fades away, downward into a dark abyss is that of Quynn, who has disappeared. Lach suffers the same fate as he is hit by Senokre, who is hit by Brenka-uku, followed by Juntor and finally Zerin who pauses in wonderment at the sudden disappearance of his friends.

"Where are you?" Zerin asks, seeking some sort of sign.

The muffled sounds of voices seem to rise from a lower level in the cave system. Zerin tries to hear better, the sounds that come from below. His efforts are interrupted as the voice of Wilber can be heard getting closer and closer.

"Where do you go? Where is my friend? Who took him? He could not have escaped by himself. There must be kidnappers on the loose. Don't go. Don't leave me, Furry. I give you nice things," says Wilber as he quickly navigates his way through the dark cave as only one with great experience can.

Zerin watches intently to see how close the deformed creature is getting, but the darkness blocks all sight. He decides he will be better to tempt whatever fate has come to his friends than to try and battle this bizarre man, blind.

Zerin steps forward onto a slippery slope and slides several feet before landing on a rough and jagged floor.

It is not as dark in here and Zerin can make out the

image of his friends, who stand to the side. He stumbles across the debris ridden floor to where they stand.

"Where are we now?" asks Zerin.

The boys take a moment to focus their eyes in this level of light. They see a dim amount of light coming from an opening, close to where they stand. They look around and then, when they focus on the ground, they see the debris that had somewhat softened their fall. Bones, and not just little bones like the ones they walked over in the first cave, these are skeletons. Many large skeletons, of animals and of humans, piled on the ground like a dump for the leftovers of some meal eaten by a savage predator.

"I do not wish to find out what placed these bones here," says Senokre.

Lach nods toward the dim light coming from the opening and says, "That is the only way out. Be ready. I believe that whatever put these bones here, lives out there."

The boys go into the opening and follow a small tunnel for a short distance. At the end of the tunnel is another opening that leads into a large room which is the source of the light.

All along the walls of this room are torches. In the center of the room is a large chair, like the throne of a king. It sits on a small stage with three steps leading down to the floor. A chain lies connected to the stage, like one for a prisoner used for entertainment. A few fresh bones lie scattered around the throne. There are piles of grass and leaves all along the sides of the walls with imprints in them like things have sat or slept on them. There are also some fresh bones around them.

"What is this place?" asks Juntor.

"Those bones beside that throne," says Quynn who pauses and swallows deeply, "they look like human bones."

Senokre points to some cloth that lies with the bones at the throne. "Look, those are the colors of the Trett scout that disappeared."

It was indeed. Whatever had taken the scout the night before had brought him back to this den and his fate was shown to him. The boys stare in anguish for a moment, caught between the thought of binding the scout for their protection and the fact that they had helped what was most likely an evil Fikron to dinner.

"We should not stay here," says Senokre. "These beds along the wall tell me there are more than one Fikron that lurks in this place, many more."

The boys look around and see an exit. The light in the den had caused them to not recognize the light coming from the opening in the den wall. They hurry to the opening and stand in the exit.

"Look," says Lach pointing to an opening at the end of the cave that leads out, back into the world where light rules the day. "It's the way out."

The boys run to the bright opening and exit the cave, into the light. Half blinded they struggle to adapt to the sun's beams which points primarily west now signaling the end of the day. As their vision clears they see that they are about halfway up the canyon wall and much further west than where they entered the first cave. The trail, on which they now stand, zigzags to the bottom. With no danger in sight, they work their way down the thin path toward the ravine floor.

At the bottom, the boys use the remaining light of the

day and travel across the ravine to get to the opposite wall, away from the caves. The further away they get from the Fikrons and that smelly Wilber, the better. As the sun disappears behind the distant terrain, the boys use the last of the light to setup camp. It has been a long day and they are ready for some rest, especially after their previous night had been shortened.

Two stand guard on the first watch while the others get some much needed rest.

Chapter 8

As the sun rises and brings life to a new day, birds fly and clouds float in the sky. A light breeze funnels through the canyon and rustles the few trees that exist along the dry river bed. It all brings a feeling of peace and safety, especially after the danger faced by the boys yesterday.

Zerin and Brenka-uku are awake, being on the last watch of the night. The rest of the boys slowly rise, one by one, with Juntor as usual, being the youngest, waking last.

Once all the boys are up and ready, Zerin calls a meeting and the boys gather around.

"We have accomplished the mission set forth by the Chimihogs. Now we have to decide what we do next," says Zerin. "Our original goal was to find Brenka-uku and return him home. If we take him home, we will forfeit our progress to this point and basically forfeit our search for Aragopia. We do have another option. We can choose not to turn back and go in search of our original goal."

"What will we do with Brenka-uku?" asks Quynn.

"Brenka and I have talked while we were on watch. He has come this far because he wants to break the tradition of fear that exists with his people. He wants to journey and find new lands, just like us. I say we continue our search for Aragopia and allow Brenka to come with us," says Zerin.

"But his family awaits his return and will be worried until then," says Senokre.

"Are our parents not worried as well?" Zerin asks and then points at Brenka-uku. "He is smaller than us, but he is about our same age, so he is as capable as us to go on this journey."

"Do you wish to go with us on this journey?" asks Lach.

"I do," answers Brenka-uku.

"So then, it is settled. What started out as three has slowly increased and of us, there are now six. Let us find then, what we set out to find, Aragopia," says Senokre with excitement.

The canyon stretches for miles toward the west and widens. Scattered along the canyon floor are medium sized rocks that must have tumbled from the upper levels of the walls of the ravine and were left and forgotten, like children's toys after the young ones had grown bored and forgotten them and thrown them to side to go play with newer ones.

There are small round bushes where the fallen stones seemed to have gathered around, as if in a meeting, or to hear what songs the bushes had to sing when the wind would blow down through the valley and give sound to the green orchestra.

The dry river bed continues its memorial to a river long since absent, weaving back and forth as if teasing the foliage that waits on its shores. Where most of the sandy soil sits and waits till the water returns so that it may continue its journey, some sand takes the offering of an occasional gust of wind to further its progression down the canyon and creates small sand dunes, like a miniature desert ready to mark its claim on the territory that seems to have been forgotten by the rains.

All along the journey, the walls, with many cave openings high and low, had stood over the boys like a menacing headmaster with many black eyes watching their every move, waiting for a mistake so that it could give the boys a good tongue lashing. Now, as the boys work their way further west, the walls back away giving more room to the travelers like they have earned the respect of the guardians of the canyon, though the tall peaks of the Pryon Mountains never waiver from their watch over the ravine and all the land as far as can be seen.

As afternoon approaches and the shadows begin to stretch away from their sources, the boys stand just after a short break and begin to make their way toward the end of the canyon. They have arrived to an area where part of the canyon continues west opening up into flat lands once again, but a portion of the canyon transforms into a ramp that curves toward the north, sloping upward toward the base of the mountains. This is the route they will have to follow, since all the stories about Aragopia say it lies on the other side of the Pryon.

Following the northward trail the boys finally exit the canyon that has controlled the better part of the last two days. Up higher now, the boys can hear more of the world that they could not hear with the massive walls that controlled what went in and out of the deep land.

One noise that comes out of nowhere, once the boys exit the canyon, is a river or waterfall that is out of sight, not too far to the west of the boys' current path. They can hear it, but cannot see it, though they are glad to know that water is close by.

As the sun begins to sink in the west, the boys set up camp again. Now on a path that runs along the base of the mountain which now stands to their east, they feel more confident, not having the sensation of being surrounded with nowhere to escape like they did inside the canyon. Just off the path, a small patch of trees provides cover and the boys enjoy the sounds of rushing water and the birds and the other peaceful sounds that are present in this place. They make a fire and sit around it. With a little time before bedtime they take the opportunity to talk.

"We have to be getting close," says Senokre. "The stories say it is just past the Pryon Mountains and here we are, right on the Pryon Mountains."

Lach turns to Brenka-uku and asks him, "Why is it that you chose to come this way? Your people seem to be very fearful of leaving the comforts of their compound. What were you looking for?"

"I had no set goal. I just wanted to explore. All my life and my father's life and his father's life were spent in that compound. I want to know more of this world," answers Brenka-uku.

"Have you heard of Aragopia, the place which we are searching?" asks Zerin.

"I have never heard of such a place, but I have never heard of any of these places outside of the compound. Only the Pryon Mountains have I ever heard of and that is only because we can see its peaks from our homes," Brenka-uku says.

"It seemed that Nork knew a lot about the history of the world and has seen many things. Did he never talk of places outside of your compound?" asks Quynn.

"He is more afraid of the outside world than my people. I have asked him questions, but he avoids them and changes the subject," says Brenka-uku.

"How long were you trapped by the stinky creature?" asks Juntor.

"I believe it was about two weeks. He had helped me find my way out of the caves and invited me for a meal. Though his smell was terrible, I was hungry and I felt I owed him some courtesy. Once I finished the meal he offered for me to stay. When I told him I had to leave, he begged me to be his friend, for he was so lonely. I told him I would keep in touch, but I had to get back to my home. He offered to guide me to the exit, but he told me the wrong way and set up a trap. I do not think he ever thought what he was doing was wrong. I think he believed that I was bad for not being his friend, so he made me be his friend. I feel sorry for him really, a wretched creature living in the darkness of the caves with no one to be his company. Oh well, there is nothing I can do. I had all intentions of visiting with him whenever I could, but he crossed the line and that is that," says Brenka-uku.

The boys sit quiet for a few moments mulling over Brenka-uku's story then Juntor chimes in again. "We ran into some cannibals who wanted to eat me. They were not too different from that creature, Wilber, for they did not believe they were in the wrong and were horrified when Lach struck down some of their men."

Brenka-uku glances at Lach and then around at all the boys and their swords which are attached to all their sides. "You all seem to be warriors or at least warriors in training. Am I correct?"

"We are. We are of the Arizz people and we learn and train at the military academy," says Senokre.

"And you killed those men that attempted to eat Juntor?" asks Brenka-uku looking at Lach.

"I did," answers Lach.

"Were you scared?" asks Brenka-uku.

"I was not. I did what a true Arizz warrior would do to evil men. I killed them because they deserved it and I would not think twice before doing it again if it was necessary," says Lach defiantly.

"We would like to find other ways to deal with bad people, but in that situation, Juntor's life was in jeopardy and Lach had no other choice. Of course Lach may disagree with me, he is a little quicker to battle than I," says Zerin.

"I admire your bravery Lach. I envy all of your military training. I wish I had that opportunity. Our people have been safe so far, but mainly because we stay confined to that little fort. I know there is more out there and I know I want to explore, but without some proper training it is very dangerous to venture out and take chances," says Brenka-uku.

"Well, while you journey with us, we can teach you some things and you can take it back to your people and maybe help them to be brave enough to explore," says Quynn. "But what do you hope to find in your adventures?"

"Everything," says Brenka-uku. "I would like to find new lands and ancient structures and treasures. As a matter of fact I found this just before I was captured by Wilber."

Brenka-uku pulls a few items out of his bag. One of the items is a medallion which catches the eye of Lach.

"That one, let me see that one," says Lach as he takes the medallion and looks it over.

The medallion is made of gold and has a few markings on it. Lach is entranced by it and stares at it long and hard as some emotion takes over his face.

"Where did you find this?" asks Lach.

"This was actually in that Fikron den that we landed in while running from Wilber. I ran across it just before I met Wilber for the first time," says Brenka-uku, who notices Lach's changing demeanor. "Have you seen it before?"

Zerin notices his friend's demeanor as well and questions him. "What is it, Lach?"

Lach takes a moment to answer and clenches the medallion tightly as he speaks. "This is the Medallion of Gokar, an heirloom of Olkar. This was passed down from generation to generation to the oldest son when he reached manhood, from his father. Olkar never received it because his father disappeared while out on a scouting mission. No one ever knew what happened to him and the medallion was lost. Olkar always feared his father was murdered by some evil that lived in the mountains."

Lach stands and looks back toward the path that they came from and says, "vengeance has been vowed on whatever took the life of Olkar's father once it was discovered who the culprit is. Now I know and since Olkar is my mentor and my guardian, and I, being the closest to a son that he has, am charged with this mission. I must leave this journey and go back to the Fikron den and kill that which has killed my mentor's father."

"Wait, wait. Slow down Lach. Let us think this over before making a rash decision," interjects Zerin. "You cannot go to fight this creature alone. You do not know how many there are and you cannot be sure they killed Olkar's father."

"I cannot sit still for a moment longer. I knew from the second I heard of the Fikron that I was meant to destroy it. Now I must go, for every breath that this creature breathes is an insult to Olkar's bloodline," says Lach.

"Please just wait till morning. It is almost dark out and it would serve you better to travel by day. Do not forget Hedgeparth's description of the Fikron's invisibility at night," says Zerin.

Lach thinks for a moment and looks around at the darkening day. "I will stay through the night, but I will not be able to sleep. I will keep watch through the night. You all may get a full night's sleep."

"Very well, it is getting time to sleep. If you decide you need a break, let me know," says Zerin.

The boys lie on their makeshift beds and one by one fall asleep, except for Lach who paces around, unable to sleep, unable to keep still. With revenge on his mind there is nothing that will deter him from his set path and anxiously he waits for first light so that he may set out to kill this creature and return the medallion to his hero and mentor, Olkar.

Early in the morning, just before the sun begins to peek over the horizon, Juntor stirs in his sleep and awakens. He looks around the makeshift camp. He stands and glances around. He notices Lach is missing. He looks around, but there is no sign of Lach so he wakes Zerin to report the news.

The conversation between the two boys awakens the others.

"What is wrong?" asks Quynn.

"Lach is missing," answers Zerin.

"Maybe he has just walked off," says Senokre. "He was very upset last night."

"Well it is too dark to look for him now. Let us wait here till there is more light. Maybe he will return," says Quynn.

So the boys settle back into their makeshift beds, except for Zerin who stands at the edge of the camp looking out into the abyss of darkness that still owns the land. The look in his eyes shows his concern. He knows Lach better than anyone else and he knows Lach isn't coming back, at least not until he conquers whatever it is he feels he has to, in order to appease his thirst for vengeance.

Later in the morning, the sun brings more light and none too soon for Zerin who stands in deep thought. One by one the boys awaken again and join Zerin.

"No sign of Lach?" asks Quynn.

"Nope," answers Zerin.

"We should go after him. If he is going after those Fikrons then he is in terrible danger," says Senokre.

"We have avoided the threat of those creatures and I do not intend on tempting it again. Besides, we are so close to our goal, it would be idiotic to turn back," says Quynn.

"But we cannot abandon him," says Senokre.

"Quynn is right. We cannot all risk the dangers of the valley and the caves again. Lach has chosen his path and he would not intend on us altering ours just for him," Zerin says.

"So we should pack our things and move on. I hope to reach Aragopia, if it exists, by tonight or tomorrow," says Quynn.

"I am torn, because I feel we should continue our journey, but I feel we should not abandon our friend though the danger is far too serious to risk," Senokre says with disappointment in his voice. "I hope he will be OK, out there alone with those creatures."

"He will not be alone," says Zerin who stares out toward the distant canyon where Lach now journeys. "I am going after him."

The boys stare at Zerin in confusion, though deep down inside they are aware of the kinship that exists between Lach and Zerin. It is one that only shows here and there, in their youth, small hints of a destiny that is to come before the end of their lifetimes.

So the boys pack their things and say their goodbyes to Zerin. They wait a moment and watch Zerin disappear into the morning mist, like a ghost crossing into another realm, a dangerous realm where only true heroes dare to venture, true heroes like Lach and Zerin, who dare to challenge the things that would scare even the bravest of warriors.

After a few moments, the boys turn toward their path, which itself is unknown as to what dangers exist between where they are and where they're going, to a land that is merely a legend that could turn out to be just a myth.

As the boys walk they have mixed emotions. They know that they are close to Aragopia or at least to finding out the truth behind the stories, but they are concerned that they may never see their longtime friends ever again. Quynn, in particular, clearly has much on his mind.

The boys walk for a few hours, now walking along the edge of the river which they had heard from their campsite. The bank of the river sits about ten feet above the actual river which rages below, far too steep for the boys to attempt to cross. A strand of large trees with low hanging limbs stand sparsely placed along the boys' path. They continue to head north searching for a calm area to cross.

At midday the boys arrive at an area of the river that widens and calms the raging waters. They stop to take a break before crossing.

As the boys sit around eating a snack they discuss what they are going to do when they find Aragopia. They laugh and smile, as it seems the hardest part of their journey is over. They enjoy the opportunity to be children for a few moments and let their worries disappear in their temporary joy, except Quynn, whose attention is often drawn away to an area in the river where the boys intend on crossing.

"Do you think Zerin has found Lach yet?" asks Juntor.

"I doubt it. Lach's seemed pretty determined to get back to that den. He's probably moving twice as fast as Zerin. When he gets determined, he thinks about nothing else, including eating and sleeping and rest," says Senokre.

"Ah, but do not underestimate Zerin when he is determined to help someone. He too will skip eating and sleeping in order to accomplish his mission," retorts Juntor.

Brenka-uku observes the two boys admirations for Lach and Zerin and asks, "It seems Lach and Zerin are a special type of human. Are there different levels of human existence? Are some humans better than others?"

"We consider all humans equal, though we all have our different abilities. Some are better at some things, while others are better at other things," Senokre says.

"But some like Lach and Zerin are so much better than others, that to me it seems some are naturally on a higher level," says Juntor.

"Do not mistake the positive attributes of a person as their only characteristics," says Quynn. "Many flawed traits can be hidden by the more noticeable good qualities of that person."

"What do you mean?" asks Senokre.

"Well, Lach for example is a great warrior and the bravest of the brave. Those are admirable traits, but they hide some of his flaws. Have you not noticed his distrust of anyone else's opinion? He is also easily seduced by revenge, which is his whole motivation for his leaving our group. That is what concerns the Mentors at the academy. Can he make wise decisions or will he be motivated by his personal desires? Only time will tell, but as for now in his youth, as superior he is as a warrior, he is inferior in his self control," states Quynn.

"I can see in Lach some of what you speak, but Zerin seems to be as great a warrior as Lach, without the lack of self control. What do you see in him as a flaw?" asks Brenka-uku.

"Zerin is actually harder to see than Lach, for Lach's

are out there to be seen as you have, Brenka. Zerin is very sensitive and his desire to do good is so great that he will accept nothing less. While a desire to do good is honorable, results aren't always going to be as one would wish. I believe that his determination to do good, could lead him to make bad choices in the pursuit of his desired result. And when he does not get this result then his original motivations could transform into revenge-like determination and lead him down a similar path as Lach," says Quynn.

A wide eyed Brenka-uku asks, "You've given this a lot of thought haven't you?"

A defiant Juntor stands and chastises Quynn. "Oh he's just jealous of Zerin. You don't know that. Zerin does good because he is good and would never do anything to hurt his people."

"Be calm Juntor. We all have special skills that have been noted by the Mentors. One of Quynn's is intelligence. What he says makes sense and I do not pretend to have a counter argument against it," Senokre says.

"So are you saying that Lach and Zerin will be as much of an obstacle as they are a benefit in this war your people are engaged in?" asks Brenka-uku.

"That is the beauty of us humans, Brenka," says Quynn. "We can overcome our flaws and be better people. We just have to recognize these flaws and work to fix them. I hope that Lach and Zerin will recognize theirs before the time comes that they are tested."

"So you are perfect?" asks Juntor mockingly.

"I have many flaws, Juntor. Some I know of and some I have yet to learn. I do know that I must strive to be a better person, because truthfully, in the end it will all eventually benefit me the most. I do not pretend to be perfect. I know that I ridicule you too much. I see your flaws and it aggravates me, but instead of being a positive influence on you, I mock you and I know better and it is something I will have to work on," says Quynn.

"So you don't mean all those things you said about me being weak and scared?" asks Juntor.

"Oh I do mean those things. I just should present it in a better way. What good is it to ridicule if you aren't going to help that person be better," Quynn says.

"Yeah you are kind of timid, Juntor," says Senokre.

"I'm tired of you guys picking on me. When we get back home, I'm going to get new friends. Friends that will treat me better," Juntor says then stands and turns his back on the boys and looks out over the horizon.

"One flaw in all of us as humans is an inability to take constructive criticism. I am as guilty as anyone, but it is an attribute of a great leader of men to take all forms of criticism, whether it nice or mean in its delivery, and make themselves a better person," Quynn says.

Juntor continues to stand with his back turned away, but his ears absorb every word.

Quynn stares back at the river with a concerned look in his face. Senokre notices and asks, "What do you see that seems to give you worry?"

"The river rages just over there, but here it is calm. It is such a short distance for it to transform this fast. It doesn't make any sense," says Quynn.

"What shall we do?" asks Brenka-uku.

"We should still cross, it is just weird, as if part of the river's power comes from another source. There is not enough water here to create such fury over there," says Quynn. "But, we must continue our journey and this is the only place to cross."

The boys gather up their things and prepare to cross the river. Senokre sees that Juntor is still angry and walks over beside him.

"Do not be angry, Juntor. We are all imperfect. All we can do is try our best. None of us will ever be perfect, but there is nothing wrong with striving to be," says Senokre. "The main thing is to try to do the right thing."

The calm area of the river is wide and shallow. It rises up to the boys knees as they wade across. The water is very clear, the debris stirred up by the raging waters now settled in its new home at the bottom of this oasis. The Pryon Mountains still tower above the boys, its snow capped tips glistening in the midday sun. Ahead, on the other side of the river awaits another wooded area with tall trees blocking any view of what lies ahead, like sentinels guarding a kingdom of great importance or maybe a land of great importance.

"Maybe this calm part of the river represents the next part of our journey, as we are clear of the raging part of the river hopefully we are clear of the raging part of our journey," says Senokre.

"Maybe so, Senokre," says Quynn.

"Maybe this is the calm before the real storm," says Juntor.

The boys roam into the thick forest that lays a few yards from the river's edge. More confident now, there is no pause but great determination, backed by their many experiences on this journey. They behave more as men and less like boys. Even if they never find this mythical land of

Aragopia, that is a worthy prize for such an amazing adventure. With no fear, as the thickness of the surrounding trees and foliage blot out the light of the day, they continue on in the dimly lit realm, getting closer and closer to the end of their journey.

After about an hour in the dense forest the boys can see more light, peeking through the trees to their right. They point and recognize the forest beginning to open and head in that direction. Excitement and anticipation grow on their faces as they know that they must be getting close to where Aragopia is said to be. Many thoughts cross their minds, of the glory of a great find, to feelings of humiliation if the sacred place is but a myth, an old man's paranoid tale. As the trees thin and the boys see open land ahead, the raging sounds of a river, hidden by the trees, grow and overtake the sounds of the forest.

"Is that another river ahead?" asks Senokre.

"I believe it is," says Quynn. "I bet it is what is feeding the other part of the river to make it so wild."

The boys walk toward the river. It becomes more visible as the forest becomes just a few thinly placed trees. Upon arrival the boys realize that the great sounds of rushing water were muffled by high banks and that the river runs wild with anger, daring anyone to cross, thirsting for its next victim. The boys stop for a moment and observe the ferocity of the water, foaming like a rabid dog waiting to attack.

"What do we do, Quynn?" asks Brenka-uku.

Quynn looks up river to the east. The water rages for as far as he can see, fed by the mountain streams. Quynn looks down river. The water bubbles and roars as it bounces off of boulders and stones, fighting with itself, as it tries to recover its path and continue its passage to whatever streams or lakes that wait.

"Do you hear that?" ask Brenka-uku.

"Hear what?" asks Quynn.

Brenka begins to walk along the shore, down the river. The boys watch. They were still getting to know their new friend and didn't know that Chimihogs have stronger senses than humans. In this case Brenka-uku's hearing can differentiate between running water and falling water. Brenka journeys along the river and just barely in the sight of the boys he finds the source of this change in sounds. It is a waterfall that falls down a cliff for about a hundred feet. Bushes and boulders block the view of the cliff from where the boys stand, but Brenka can see clearly and peeks through the brush. He signals the boys to come to him.

"What do you see?" asks Juntor as the boys close in on Brenka-uku.

"Come look," says Brenka-uku.

The boys peek through to see a magnificent waterfall. The water doesn't fall straight down, it leaps off of the top of the cliff like it is diving into the pool below, then after a few minutes to recover, as if waiting on its turn to get in line, then begins to rush down the river again.

Brenka-uku points down the cliff. Beside the waterfall the land is not as steep and trees grow on the slant of the cliff side. "See, we can work our way down here and maybe we can find a shallow place to cross."

The boys agree and slowly work their way down the cliff, tying makeshift ropes to the trees to help them in their descent. The waterfall rages beside them, every once in a while a stray splash of water catches them off guard.

Finally they reach the bottom and look around. They check the depth of the pool just outside of the splash of the falling water, but it is too deep. They work their way a little farther down river to a calmer spot and check the depth again, but it is far too deep to cross. They continue to walk along the river bank, stopping every few hundred yards, checking the depth, still coming up with the same disappointing news. It is too deep.

Quynn stops and says, "If we continue like this, by the time we find a place shallow enough to cross, we'll be halfway back home. Let us stop for a moment to discuss a game plan."

The boys pause, each taking a seat and taking a moment to catch their breath after the climb down the high cliff. They sit and think, silent. Something catches Brenka-uku's eye a ways down the river. As with very good hearing, he also has very good eye site and he focuses in on something.

Quynn notices the Chimihog staring and asks him, "what do you see, Brenka?"

"I think I see something spread across the river up ahead," he responds.

Brenka-uku gets up and walks toward this thing. The boys get up and follow him. As they close in they see what he saw. It is a bridge made of rope, crossing the river. They all run over to the bridge.

After a closer look at the rope bridge the boys pause and consider their options. To see something from far off does not tell the whole truth about it. Sometimes it is better than imagined and sometimes it is worse than hoped for. In this case, this bridge was good from afar, but far from good.

Clearly this was an ancient bridge. It had one rope running across as a place for your feet. Then two ropes ran above it for holding on. Several small ropes connected the two top ropes to the bottom rope, creating a V-shaped, shaky passage across the raging, deep river. And that was when it was brand new. Now the ropes are frayed and many of the connecting ropes are rotted or broken. The right side top rope has much more slack in it than does the left side top rope. The river must have risen over the years, because the bottom rope dips a few inches into the passing water near the middle of the bridge.

The boys stare silently at the ancient crossing. Senokre grabs the top right rope and shakes it. Brenka-uku looks further down river, hoping to find another option for crossing to the other side.

After a few moments, Quynn speaks. "Here we are. This seems to be our only option for crossing. Who goes first?"

The boys all look at Quynn in horror and he laughs.

"Come on warriors, after all we've been through, don't let this be the obstacle that turns us from our goal," says Quynn.

"I am not afraid. It's just that I can fight enemies. I cannot fight water," says Senokre.

"This bridge will hold," says Quynn. "We just need to cross it one at time."

The boys observe the bridge and its ropes. They examine the rushing waters below. All are timid, but they will not be denied finishing their journey. Quynn watches the expressions and mannerisms of his younger colleagues.

"I will go first," he says.

The boys' shoulders relax as sighs of relief seep from their mouths like a tire pierced by a blade. Quynn laughs again.

"Do not be so relieved, as each one of us will carry the burden of safely crossing this bridge," says Quynn.

Quynn steps to the edge of the bridge and studies it. The ropes seem secure along this side of the river, secured by a tree and stones. Quynn observes the ropes crossing the bridge with his eyes. It goes about a eighty feet to the other side. On the other side the ropes seem to be secured to trees and stones in the same way. About ten feet below the embankment at the rope bridge's end, along the river's edge, is a raised area of land, creating a shore extending out from the river bank about thirty or so feet before being taken over by the river. This gives Quynn a little comfort, because if he can make it at least that far, then if he happens to fall, the shore may give him a second chance to prevent from being swept away by the currents.

He puts one foot on the bridge and grabs the two top ropes with his hands. He slowly places weight on the bridge and bounces a little. It holds. Quynn takes a deep breath and begins the long slow journey across, testing the stability along the way. The bridge is very shaky and more than once Quynn is forced to stop and regain his balance, and his composure. In the middle, where the water washes over the bottom rope, Quynn has to hold extra tight. The pressure of the running water is more than he had anticipated, but he pulls through. The other boys watch intensely. As Quynn closes in over top of the exposed land below the bridge, his tensions ease a little and he speeds up his pace across the bridge, until he reaches the end and half excited and half determined to be free of the ragged bridge, he leaps to the land on the other side and looks back triumphantly at the others.

"That was nothing. What are you waiting for?" he taunts then turns so that the boys can't see him and takes a big sigh of relief.

The boys stand looking at each other. No one is eager to volunteer.

Then Senokre steps forward. "I will go next."

He steps forward and grabs the ropes, takes a first step, tests the sturdiness and then slowly makes the shaky trip across the bridge.

"Be careful at that middle part. The current is strong. Keep a tight hold," Quynn says as he coaches Senokre across.

Senokre finally reaches the other side and is greeted by Quynn, who seems as excited about Senokre's successful crossing as he was about his own.

"Next," says Quynn.

Juntor looks at Brenka-uku and says, "Will you please go next? I am going to cross, but I am scared and I don't want them to know. I just need a little more time to get my nerve up. If you volunteer to go first then there will be no debate and I won't have to hear Quynn ridicule me. I'm just so tired of him trying to make me look like a coward and an immature child."

Brenka-uku places his hand on Juntor's shoulder and nods then turns toward the bridge. He follows suit and grabs the ropes tightly, slowly feeling out the bridge with each step. He takes a few steps, then stops suddenly and looks into the water.

"What is it?" shouts Quynn from the other side.

"It was nothing. I just thought I saw something in the

water," says Brenka-uku.

Brenka-uku continues along the bridge and arrives close to the middle, where the water still rushes across and the bottom rope almost disappears from sight. He stops. Something in the water catches his sight again. The boys watch from each side of the river. Brenka-uku observes the water for a moment then moves slowly forward, his eyes still on the river below. He steps into the water having to feel now for the bottom rope. The water splashes around his lower legs. Brenka-uku takes another step and feels around to get a good footing on the bridge. Suddenly, in a flash, with reflexes never before seen in the human world, Brenka-uku swings himself out of the water, supporting his weight by his arms only, as a white colored alligator-like creature lunges at the water covered area of the bridge. Just missing, but still in attack mode, the white alligator, called an Albinogator, rips at the bottom rope.

"Watch out Brenka," says Quynn. "There is another one."

Chapter 9

The fog is heavy, as if the clouds have lowered to give Zerin some cover so he may not be detected by a Fikron, or any other evil that may exist in the canyon. Luckily for Zerin, he is somewhat familiar with the terrain, having been through only a few days earlier. He cautiously walks along with his sword drawn.

Suddenly through the dirty white mist, Zerin sees a black image moving in the distance, followed by another. Two Fikrons roam just ahead of Zerin as if hunting, hunting perhaps for some young boys who are a long way from home.

"Fikrons," Zerin whispers to himself.

Zerin squats down and turns his direction from eastward now north, toward the edge of the canyon, till he reaches the steep wall of the ravine. The mist blinds Zerin from seeing how high the wall rises, but he cannot go forward and he will not turn back. Whether the canyon wall rises a few feet or several hundred, he must scale the rock wall to the top and try to take the higher route to where he believes Lach to be heading.

Slowly Zerin works his way up the wall as he tests gripping points and then pulls himself up. Occasionally slipping and having to desperately claw at the wall to find another grip, he doggedly pushes on. The wall is high, or maybe the ascent is slow, but now below Zerin seems to be a bottomless pit filled with the dirty white fog. Zerin pauses and takes a deep breath, just enough to summon up a little more strength for his will, he continues on.

Sweating and panting, Zerin searches above with his right hand for a new grip. His legs tremble as they struggle to hold his weight on tiny notches in the wall. His breathing increases as his frustration grows, fueled by his approaching muscle failure. He gets angry and in his adrenaline fed rage, he reaches as high as he possibly can and feels the top. He grips as tight as he can and pulls himself up and over with the last bit of energy in his body. He rolls over on his back, and laughs while he tries to catch his breath, joy overtaking fatigue.

"You're going to owe me big time after this, Lach," Zerin says as he lays there.

The sun lightens up the sky as the fog begins to dissipate. Zerin walks along a natural road of flat land between the bottom of the mountains and the edge of the canyon. Mostly barren, there are occasional small bushes and patches of grass. The bottom of the canyon takes on a different appearance from above and Zerin can look out over all of the vast low land. He can also see the occasional black dot roaming the canyon floor.

"Hopefully Fikrons cannot climb," Zerin says with a smile.

Zerin uses his positions above the canyon to try to catch a possible glimpse of Lach.

Zerin walks along staring down into the wide ravine and doesn't even notice an indentation in the mountain side that lies ahead. A noise, like the chatter of people, catches his attention. He looks forward and sees what seems to be a wagon. He moves quickly to a nearby bush at the edge of the mountain wall and ducks behind, in order to observe this wagon in such a strange location.

The wagon sits alone, but the sounds of the goings on of a village warn Zerin that the wagon is not an abandoned remnant of a past civilization.

A few more moments pass by and Zerin decides to move closer. He uses the edge of the mountain as a wall to hide his approach. Finally reaching the opening in the mountain side, he positions himself at a bush that lies at the corner and peeks over.

It is a small village built inside of a large gap in the mountain. The villagers appear to be human, but there clothing is old and worn, having the style of long ago. The village also has an ancient design. The buildings appear to have been around for centuries. The people carry on through the small village like any other village. Children play, old women cook by fires and clean, and men trade and barter.

Zerin continues to study the people while he considers

if he should just pass by or meet with them and perhaps learn of any news on Lach.

"Who are you?" asks a young boy who has snuck up on Zerin.

The little boy is probably about six years old. He shows no signs of fear by the presence of Zerin, and stands right next to him.

"Um, I am Zerin," Zerin says as he pauses in search of something to say. "Who are you?"

"I am Yatique et Vaugne," answers the young boy. "Your clothes are strange. Where are you from?"

"I am from the land of the Arizz, a large kingdom to the south," answers Zerin.

The little boy looks away from Zerin, toward the village. Zerin, still hidden by the bush, looks in the same direction to see an older woman walking in his direction.

"Yatique, what are you doing out here?" she questions the young boy as she gets closer. "You know it is dangerous for a young child to be outside of the mountain wall. The Fikron are out and about and you know we all must be careful."

"We have a visitor," says Yatique pointing behind the bush where Zerin still squats.

The old lady stops in her tracks.

"What visitor, Yatique?"

"Stand Zerin et Arizz, introduce yourself," says Yatique as he tugs at Zerin's arm.

Zerin takes a deep breath and stands.

The old lady stares at him for a second, studying him with distrust in her eyes.

She eyes his sword and asks, "Who are you and what

are you doing here?"

"I am Zerin and I am searching for my friend who has gone on a mission alone. I must find him," he says.

"How old are you?" she asks.

"I am twelve years old, but do not let my age fool you. I am a well trained warrior of the Arizz," states Zerin.

"Where is your friend?" the old lady asks.

"I believe him to be down in that canyon searching for...," Zerin pauses.

The old lady seems to know what he was about to say and she anxiously looks in both directions outside of the cave wall, then says, "It is not safe out here. Let us go into the village and we can talk more."

The old lady leads Zerin and Yatique into the boundaries of the village. The people stare at Zerin with curiosity. There is no fear of him, because being only twelve years old can have its advantages.

The old lady leads them to a central structure which has three walls and roof, with a large opening where the fourth wall would have been. It is made up of a thin bamboo-like material, allowing plenty of light through the loosely bound siding.

Inside several people go about their business. There are a few old men that sit in a corner debating and playing some sort of card game.

"Wait here," says the old lady as she walks into the structure.

While Zerin waits, he glances around the village. The huts that surround the central structure sit throughout, all the way up to the edge of the mountain sides. The village has an upward slant, with the huts closest to the mountains walls being on a slightly higher elevation. It is not a big area, but it is secure. A few strange, large trees grow in the village, like a rare species that only grow in such an unusual location. The back mountain wall of the village rises almost straight up, hundreds of feet. It is like a village from a long lost history, forgotten by time, but thriving on with little or no contact with the outside world.

"Come in young man," says one of the old men who were debating in the corner.

Zerin walks into the structure and takes a seat with the old men. Yatique follows him in and sits on the floor near the meeting.

"I am Mareege et Vaugne," says the old man that called him in. "Welcome to our village of Vaugne.

"I am Zerin."

"Jirick says that you are of the Arizz tribe," says Mareege pointing to the old lady.

"Yes, I am Arizz," answers Zerin.

"It has been a long time since I have seen an Arizz. I was only a little boy. But our people are weary of war and the Arizz seem to never grow tired of war, so we stopped communicating with all the tribes," says Mareege.

"There are only two tribes now," says Zerin, "the Arizz and the Trett."

"Only two tribes, the rest destroyed by war, no?" asks Mareege.

"I do not know. There have been many wars in the past, but history is a hard thing to learn, I am finding out," says Zerin.

"Are your people at war with the Trett?" asks Mareege.

"The Trett are led by an evil leader who betrayed the Arizz long ago," says Zerin.

"It only takes one evil man to turn a mass of people against each other," says Mareege. "This is why we avoid contact with the outside. People are different and don't always agree on things, but rather than working together or at least separating themselves so as avoid any growing tensions, they would rather conquer those who they disagree with so as to push their ways onto them. This of course causes retaliation, and before you know it, neither side knows why they started fighting and just fight because the other group is 'the enemy'.

I do not pretend to have answer to this problem, but I know there has to be a better way. Though, you see, I cannot tell someone they are wrong if I, myself, cannot present a solution. I could say peace, but peace isn't always achieved by laying down weapons, for we are a peaceful people, but if we are attacked, we have the means and will fight back and defend ourselves.

I am an old man and I have seen a lot of things. I am considered wise by my people, but as for the subject of war and peace, I have no answer. I can only hope that you can take my words and add them to the knowledge you gain as you go through life, and maybe you will be the one with the right answers, if ever a young man meets with you when you are old and wise."

Zerin smiles and nods at the old man's words.

"It is getting late. I do not wish to aggravate your ears any more than I have. I am just an opinionated old man and do not intend to insult your people, because no matter what tribe we are from, we are all brethren and therefore more the same than different. You are young and still have much to learn, but as I look into your eyes I see you are very wise for your age," says Mareege.

"You must be hungry. We have food for you, follow me and I will show you where you can sleep tonight," says Jirick who takes his hand and leads him away.

Zerin stops and turns back toward Mareege. "Thank you for your counsel. I will leave first thing in the morning. My friend is out there and I must go stand by his side."

"I would ask you to avoid the Fikron and take a different route home, but I see your mind is made up and you are loyal to your friend. So I say good luck and may good overcome evil," states Mareege.

Zerin nods and follows Jirick, followed by little Yatique.

Chapter 10

Brenka-uku struggles to support himself on the two top ropes, with his legs sprawled out over the ropes and his hands as his primary support. He slips as the Albinogator shakes the whole bridge with its lashing. Brenka-uku loses his grip on the right side rope and partially falls into the water, holding on for dear life. The Albinogator releases the rope, now realizing its mistake. Another Albinogator lunges at the fallen Chimihog, but with his amazing reflexes on display again, he dodges the attack and manages to get above the water on the top ropes once more.

More Albinogators are drawn to the bridge by the commotion and swarm the water just below the Chimihog. An Albinogator lunges out of the water, but the white beasts are not built to leap upward and it cannot reach Brenka-uku on the top ropes.

"Come on Brenka," yells Quynn. "They cannot reach you, move, move."

Brenka-uku wriggles across the top ropes, like a worm crossing a limb. All along the Albinogators lunge, unsuccessfully, out of the water. He reaches the other side and swings to safety, but is visibly shaken. He places his hands on his knees to get control of his breath. Quynn and Senokre check on him and see if he is OK. For a moment they forget about Juntor. Quynn remembers first and looks across at the frightened young boy.

Fear covers Juntor's face in pale white, as if all the life has already left his body. This wasn't the first time Quynn had seen Juntor like this. A few times in the past, after a run in with his drunken father, Juntor could be seen walking alone through the city with the deathly look on his face. Quynn wasn't sure if they would be able to get Juntor to cross the rope. Many had tried to get him to stand up to his father, but some things are mental and when something gets into your head, it is very hard to get it out.

"Juntor," Quynn calls.

Juntor does not respond.

"Juntor, if you cross on the top rope like Brenka-uku did, they cannot get you," Quynn says.

"I can't," yells Juntor.

"Yes you can, Juntor," answers Quynn.

"I can't," says Juntor with a quiver in his voice.

"Come on Juntor, cross the bridge. Don't be a baby," says Quynn.

Juntor just stares at the Albinogators which wait

patiently for someone else to cross the bridge. He says to himself, "I can't."

"Cross the bridge, now! We are almost there. We can't leave you here. You have to cross," says Quynn.

Quynn gets angry and turns to Brenka-uku and Senokre and says, "He can cross the bridge safely if he stays on the top rope. I knew it was a bad idea for him to come."

Juntor watches from the other side, seeing Quynn flail his arms around, knowing that Quynn was talking bad about him.

"Go on without me. I'll try to make my way back home. I know you don't want me here anyway," says Juntor.

Quynn bites his lip and tenses up. "You can cross the bridge, Juntor. Cross the bridge," he yells.

Juntor stands silent with defeat and shame on his face. Quynn stands and watches him, getting more and more agitated. Finally Quynn has all he can take.

"Go on then. You have been a problem since we started. You are no warrior. You are just a boy. Grow up, Juntor," says Quynn.

"Shut up Quynn. I'm tired of your insults. You are not better than me and I'm not going to take it anymore. I don't need you. I don't need any of you," Juntor yells as he paces back and forth on the riverbank, the white fear in his face, now transformed into red anger. He walks away from the bridge and sits under a tree a little ways from the riverbank.

Quynn looks at Brenka-uku. Senokre stands silent.

"He can do it if he will just try. But he is too hard headed," says Quynn.

"He can do it, but he needs support, not ridicule," says

Brenka-uku.

"He won't listen to me," says Quynn.

"Do you remember earlier when you were talking about working on our faults, and trying to be better people?" asks Brenka-uku.

Quynn thinks for a minute, sighs then nods his head.

"It has been said that you are to be leader. It has been said that he is to be a brave warrior. Perhaps his success in achieving such lies in your success. When you start leading, perhaps he will start being brave," Brenka-uku says.

Quynn takes a deep breath and nods his head. He looks at the rope bridge and the river and the Albinogators lurking below. He goes to the bridge, positions himself on the top ropes and works his way across. The ropes shake, the water rages and the Albinogators lunge, but Quynn works his way across to the other side.

Juntor frowns as he watches Quynn cross. He wonders what Quynn is up to. Is he showing him it can be done, or is he so mad that he would cross a raging river full of bloodthirsty creatures, just to beat him up? As Quynn arrives to Juntor's side, Juntor stands up.

Brenka-uku and Senokre watch from the other side as Quynn gets across the bridge and walks to Juntor. They can see Juntor shouting at Quynn and Quynn waving his hands back and forth. Senokre gets concerned for a moment that the two may come to blows as the argument gets more and more heated. The discussion seems to simmer down then Juntor walks to the bridge. Quynn follows and puts his arm on Juntor's shoulder, but Juntor shrugs it off. Juntor gets on the top ropes and fearfully, but defiantly works his way across the shaky ropes. As he reaches the middle and the lowest point, the Albinogators lunge, and the fear comes back into his face. Quynn coaches him from the other side as Senokre and Brenka-uku urge him on.

"You are doing good Juntor. Keep moving, almost there," says Quynn.

Juntor finally reaches the other side, and is helped off by Senokre and Brenka-uku, but no one notices one of the top ropes tears a little as he exits. Now Quynn must cross again.

"Are you OK?" Senokre asks Juntor. "What did he say to you?"

"I don't really know. Basically, he was lecturing me," says Juntor.

"Was he mean to you?" asks Brenka-uku.

"I'm just tired of him lecturing me, like I am a baby. I already have one father and he isn't much to be proud of, I don't need another," says Juntor.

As the boys talk, they keep an eye on Quynn who has reached the most dangerous part of the bridge. The Albinogators lunge out of the water, often bumping in to each other now that there are so many lurking below. The occasional scuffle breaks out as Albinogators do have short tempers. They all keep their eyes on the potential meal that dangles above them, so close but so far away. Quynn patiently and bravely continues across the rope bridge slowly, but determined. His arms burn and his grip struggles. The rope that has more slack makes it much more difficult to balance and for some reason it seems to be getting looser.

On the river bank the boys continue to talk.

"You know sometimes we can hear the way someone speaks to us and completely miss what they are telling us. One thing I have learned from Nork is to take even the words of your enemy to heart and consider them, for those words can be used to your benefit, even if it is against that enemy. In this case of course, I guarantee you that Quynn's words to you were for your good. Take a moment to let go of your anger with him and think about his words only," says Brenka-uku.

Juntor thinks about Brenka-uku's words, nods then walks away thinking about this new way of looking at things.

Senokre looks at Brenka-uku amazed and says, "You really say some wise things for being around the same age as us."

"It is the wisdom of Nork. Weekly we sit around with him and he teaches us all that he knows," says Brenka-uku.

Senokre thinks about Nork for a second, but only a second because a rip and a scream claim everyone's attention. The boys look toward Quynn.

The right side rope has broken and Quynn desperately holds on to the left side rope, struggling to keep his lower body raised out of the water, out of the reach of the Albinogators. Now about three quarters of the way, his body shakes as his energy saps and his arms burn so much that his grip begins to fail. The Albinogators lunge upward trying to snatch onto Quynn's legs as they drop into range then raise back out of danger with every move he makes toward land.

"Keep coming, Quynn, you are almost here," shouts Senokre, desperately trying to motivate his friend.

Juntor who had walked a little ways off runs back over to see Quynn's dilemma. Just then, an Albinogator times Quynn's movements and latches on to the heel of Quynn's boot. Quynn pulls himself just to the edge of the lower shore below the bridge and for a split second his eyes locks with

Juntor and Juntor sees the fear in his eyes as Quynn's grip finally fails him and he falls into the river's edge.

The boys scream from the riverbank and watch in horror as Quynn disappears under the water, but within a split second, Quynn emerges from the water, leaping onto the lower shore. There is blood on his leg.

"He is injured," says Senokre.

The boys watch for a moment more and realize that the blood is the blood of the Albinogator that bit his boot. Quynn desperately crawls onto the lower shore and is immediately surrounded by several ravenous Albinogators who follow him out of the water onto the small piece of land. He stands, sword drawn in full warrior mindset. One of the predators lunges for Quynn. He strikes it down, dead with a piercing stab to the head.

The boys stand above, frozen with fear for their friend as he battles an ever increasing number of Albinogators flooding the land mass below. Juntor looks at his two companions.

"We have to help him," he says. His words go unnoticed by the two fearful youth.

Senokre and Brenka-uku continue to watch in horror, their hands on their sword ready to strike, but the terror in their bodies will not let them move. In both of their minds the thought is, "if only Lach and Zerin were here."

Suddenly, while Quynn's attention is on defending against two of the reptilian attackers, another clamps down on his leg from behind. He screams in pain and terror. Will this be his end? There are far too many for him to fend off on his own. He fights on, undeterred.

A yell and a triumphant shout changes the sounds of

the moment and as Senokre looks toward the source of the noise, he sees out of the corner of his eye, someone leap into the pit of Albinogators, sword drawn stabbing one through its eyeball then immediately attacking another. Was this Zerin or Lach returning to save the day? Senokre focuses on the hero and sees that it is Juntor, looking not like a scared little boy, but a mature warrior. Senokre and Brenka-uku look at each other for a second and with a shout they plunge, swords drawn, into the melee.

The primitive skills of the Albinogators are no match for the well trained youth. The fear that was in the boys trades its allegiance and takes over the Albinogators. The white scales of the creatures turn red as their own blood and the blood of their brothers spatters about. Slowly, many of the Albinogators begin to retreat into the once foamy white waters of the river, now red like wine being washed away.

Juntor kills the last aggressive gator and the remaining predators follow their retreating comrades. The boys stand for a moment, panting and covered in Albinogator blood with their warrior faces still on.

After a moment they look around at the surrounding carnage and at each other. Smiles begin to show up on their faces and shouts of victory follow. The boys high five and bump forearms and hug and jump around. They have survived.

After some cautious rinsing at the edge of the river and with most of the blood washed away, they climb out of the river bed.

Once everyone is out they continue their journey. A long while they walk without saying a word. They are all deep in their minds, reliving the riveting battle.

Juntor carries himself noticeably different. A new sense of confidence shows in his expression. He can stand proud beside the likes of Lach and Zerin and his other youth warriors as a deserving member.

Quynn also walks proud, knowing that his words had made a difference in the youngest of the group's life.

The day begins to come to its end. The boys can see an opening in the forest, perhaps the exit. But the day has been long and they are too tired to venture any further. They stop while there is still light and set up camp.

The campfire lights the boys' faces as they sit around, eating on some gator meat. Senokre had cut up some pieces while they were cleaning up back at the river and it helps fill their stomachs. A lot of energy it takes, when battling for your life.

Quynn and Juntor did not speak about their personal achievements and their better understanding of their relationship, but it didn't need words. They just knew. More interesting topics commanded all their attention.

"We have to be close, if Aragopia exists," says Senokre.

"I enjoy adventure, but I do not know how much more of this excitement I can take. Back there, that was a close call," says Brenka-uku.

"How's your leg, Quynn?" asks Senokre.

"I'll make it. There are two teeth marks that went pretty deep, but I think my boot helped stop some of the damage. I do hope we find something soon though. I would like to rest for a few days. I feel like Brenka, I'm ready for a break from this excitement," says Quynn.

"According to all that I've ever learned about Aragopia, it has to be very close. As much as I would like to find this land, I must say, if we do not find it tomorrow, we should consider heading home," says Senokre.

"You are right. You have families that are worried by now and shouldn't be troubled much longer. I agree, if we do not find Aragopia tomorrow, then we can go back with our heads high and tell everyone that we searched for the legend and it turned out to only be a myth," says Quynn, but then he leans in close to the fire and says, "But I believe it exists and I believe it is just past the opening of this forest."

Juntor thinks for a moment then looks at Quynn and says, "You said 'You have families to go home to', not 'We'."

Quynn shakes his head and says. "No I didn't, did I? Maybe I did. I meant to say 'We'. Oh well, it's been a long day. I am probably just tired."

The boys continue talking, but Juntor feels there is more to the mistake than Quynn just being tired and he takes his concern to bed with him. All the boys finally fall asleep and say goodbye to a long day.

A mist shrouds the forest as morning has come and the boys are slowly working their way to the forest edge. Quynn's leg has taken a turn for the worse overnight and he struggles to keep up, even with their slow pace.

The mist begins to thicken to a point where they can no longer see the edge of the woods. They continue, blindly, in the direction that they believe will lead to the end of the mass of trees.

"This fog is so thick. I have almost run into three trees

already," Senokre says.

The boys walk on. After a while Brenka-uku pauses and looks around. He sticks his arms out, waving them as if he is feeling for something. He moves in a circle while he continues to feel around. The other boys do not see him, as the fog is so thick they that can no longer see one another.

Brenka-uku yells out, "I do not believe we are in the forest anymore. I haven't seen a tree in a while."

"Where are you Brenka? You sound far away," Juntor says.

"How can we know where he is? I can hear you right beside me and I still cannot see you, Juntor," says Senokre

"Brenka is right. I believe we have exited the forest. We need to gather back together and figure out what to do. Brenka, I am going to whistle. I want you to find your way to me. You two should probably try to follow my whistle, too. This fog may be tricking us in believing we are closer than we really are," says Quynn.

Quynn whistles and the others try to get close enough to at least see the images of each other. Juntor is first. He was only a few feet away from Quynn. Senokre is not far behind. The boys wait on Brenka. The Chimihog occasionally calls out to let the boys know how far he is away. The process takes some time. Basically Brenka-uku is walking blind and the boys are calling for him blindly. Finally he bumps into Juntor and the boys let out groans and then laugh at each other's mistake.

"Where are we?" asks Juntor.

"This is a very heavy fog. It seems like it might be dangerous for us to continue until it clears up a little," says Senokre. "What do you think Quynn?"

Quynn does not answer. What the boys are unable to see in the dense fog is that Quynn's wound has begun to affect his entire body and his face has become pale and sickly.

"Quynn?" calls Senokre.

There is a moment of silence then there is a thud. In the blurred view of the boys they see the shape of Quynn lying on the ground.

"What was that?" asks Brenka-uku.

"Quynn has fallen," says Senokre as he rushes to the eldest's side.

"Are you OK?" he asks Quynn as he kneels beside him.

Quynn lies on the ground, awake but confused and dazed.

"Quynn, Quynn, are you OK?" asks Senokre.

Quynn looks up at Senokre, still a little dazed. Senokre looks closely at him and sees what the fog had covered. Quynn is very sick, his wound now infected.

"My leg hurts. It is throbbing and I can barely move it," says Quynn.

Quynn's leg is swollen and the wound has opened up due to the swelling. A greenish ooze drips from the large hole in his leg and the skin around the wound has a darkened color, like a small volcano that has erupted green lava. Senokre is startled after his examination of Quynn's extremity.

"We have to get you some medicine. Your leg needs some immediate attention," says Senokre.

"What do we do, Senokre? We can't see more than a foot in front of us," Juntor says.

"And if we continue, we do not know where we are going. We can't see to know if we are getting closer to help, or further away," says Brenka-uku.

Quynn lets out a stressed moan as the pain in his leg grows to an intolerable level.

It subsides after a few moments and Quynn says, "The pain in my leg is growing. It comes in waves, but each gets more and more painful."

"Where is Aragopia? According to your friend, it should be right around here, Senokre," says Juntor.

"Come help me get Quynn up. We must move. We need to find our way out of this mess," says Senokre.

Brenka-uku helps Senokre pull Quynn up. Quynn stands for a moment, but begins to sway.

"I am dizzy," says Quynn who then drops to one knee. "I feel as if I am going in and out of consciousness. I do not even remember how I got to standing."

Quynn speaks to himself a few times, saying strange things that make no sense.

"What did you say, Quynn?" asks Juntor.

"What? I did not say anything," says Quynn as he begins to groan again. A wave of pain overtakes him.

"We have to get him help," says Juntor.

"But which way do we go?" asks Brenka-uku.

Senokre thinks for a moment. He turns to Quynn and asks, "Can you walk any at all?"

"Yes," says Quynn. "Of course I can walk."

Senokre helps Quynn to his feet. Quynn stumbles and Senokre places Quynn's arm over his shoulder and attempts to help the sick boy walk.

"Let us walk as far as we can. I do not know how

much longer his body can take this infection," says Senokre.

"Which way?" asks Juntor.

"I don't know, just start walking!" yells Senokre.

The boys do not get far until Senokre is supporting the entire weight of Quynn. His legs drag alongside Senokre's, who now pants for breath, fatigued by the burden. Finally, both Senokre and Quynn fall.

"I need help," says Senokre. "I cannot carry him alone."

Juntor grabs Quynn's other arm and Brenka-uku grabs Quynn's legs. Senokre catches his breath and takes back a hold of Quynn's arm. The three boys begin to awkwardly carry their ailing friend.

"Quynn, how are you doing?" asks Brenka-uku.

"He's unconscious right now. He goes in and out. He is getting worse," says Senokre.

The boys stumble along, carrying their load. Their breathing steadily increasing as fatigue begins to creep into their muscles. Slowly moans and groans begin to escape the boy's mouths. The load is heavy and the pace is slow and the fog is not clearing. Like the haze that clouds Quynn's failing mind the relentless mist lead the boys' thoughts into the unknown. Their hope begins to fail.

Slower and slower the boys move along until finally Senokre trips and tumbles to the ground causing a chain reaction which pulls all the boys to the ground. They sit up from their fall and struggle to regain their breath. Quynn writhes in pain then passes out again. Juntor lets out a frustrated growl.

"He is going to die and we are stuck here, with no way of helping him. He is going to die and we are on this ridiculous journey to find a land from children's stories. I wish I never came to this place. I hate that I ever heard of Aragopia. He is going to die and we are stuck in the foggy nowhere land, where we will probably die, too. Why did we come on this journey?" asks Juntor.

"We can't give up," says Brenka-uku.

"We are not giving up. It is just, what do we do? It is like a fog has taken over the land and there is no direction. Like a desert of gray mist, no matter how far we travel, all that there is, is just fog," says Senokre.

"Look at his leg," says Juntor.

Quynn's whole leg is now swollen, from his foot to his thigh. Its dark purplish color in the thick fog makes it look more like the fallen trunk of a tree than a leg. His face is almost completely white and death appears to be inching its way in.

"All is lost," says Juntor. "We should have stayed with Zerin. Now we have to watch our friend die right beside us."

Quynn comes to and looks up at Senokre and says, "The pain has stopped."

Senokre looks down at Quynn's leg. It is worse than ever.

"Is it better?" asks Quynn.

Senokre stays silent, but a few tears run from his eyes. Quynn notices.

"I guess I'm dying," he says. "I must be dying."

"I am sorry for dragging you on this stupid adventure. I really believed that Aragopia existed. Now we know it was just a stupid dream. Now we will all pay for my stupidity," says Senokre.

Juntor and Brenka-uku sit sobbing as the reality of their situation sets in more and more.

"All is lost, Juntor. I believe you are right. I am sorry," says Senokre as he lowers his head and cries.

The boys sit, devastated and lost. Their images blurred by the ever present gray fog. The image of Quynn lying on the ground is a spooky sign of the possible end that is to come for all the young adventurers. Time seems to stop and all that is, is grayness.

A voice ruptures the silence. "Who goes there?" asks the voice with a slightly British accent.

Chapter 11

The boys perk up. Their senses heighten due to their inability to see.

"Who goes there, I says," the voice demands, this time a little louder.

The boys stand and draw their swords, all but Quynn who lies in a near comatose state.

"I do believe the boys may be deaf," says another voice with a more gruff tone.

"We hear you, we just do not see you," says Senokre.

"Oh, perhaps they are blind, not deaf, as you accuse," says the first voice to the second voice.

"We are neither blind, nor deaf, but are unable to see through this thick haze," says Senokre.

The two voices snicker.

"They do not know. They do not realize," says the gruff voice.

"What we do and do not realize doesn't matter. It is best that you realize who we are and what we are capable of when a threat is brought against us," Juntor says, defiantly, mimicking Lach.

"Now calm down there youngster. We mean you no harm," says the first voice.

Footsteps get closer and closer to the boys.

"Your friend seems to not be very well," says the gruff voice.

"How do you see so well in this fog?" asks Brenka-uku.

The two voices laugh and then the gruff voice says, "I told you."

"There is no fog my young friend. Your eyes might be open, but you mind is closed so that you may not see all that there is to see," says the first voice.

"Would you stop speaking in riddles? If you are not intending on harming us and you see our friend is very sick, then help us," says Senokre.

"My apologies, though I am still wondering why four youngsters are so far from their homes," says the first voice.

"We set out to find a place that was told to us by a crazy old man. We set out to find the mythical land of Aragopia, but now it seems that it does not exist and we are lost," says Senokre.

"So you set out to find this mythical land and it seems your mission has failed? Do you no longer believe that Aragopia exists?" asks the gruff voice.

"We just want to go home and get our friend some help. Obviously Aragopia was just a big lie and now we suffer for our ignorance," says Senokre.

"You are right. You do suffer because of your ignorance, but not in your belief in your adventure. You suffer because of your doubt in the existence of such a place," says the first voice.

"We did believe, but as you can see there is nothing here", says Brenka-uku.

"What I see is different from what you see. It is easy to become cynical and lose faith in something you cannot see, especially in the face of adversity. It is not where you are, but where your mind is that determines the existence of such places. It is not a fog that blocks your sight, but a doubt that blocks your mind. Now close your eyes young ones," says the first voice.

The boys close their eyes, having no other options. All that burdens them feels like a huge weight holding their bodies down, as if the mist itself was solid like a heavy blanket wrapped tightly around their bodies. The burden clouds their minds with doubts and concern.

"I cannot clear my mind. All that I see and feel is despair," says Senokre.

"Believe as you did when you started this journey. Put away all these new burdens and free your mind of your doubt," says one voice.

The boys focus and try to follow the directions of the strangers which they cannot see. All the burden stands in their minds, fighting for control as the boys try to bring hope back into their heads.

The training that the young boys have had at the

academy begins to show and they begin to clear the bad thoughts from their minds. They start to feel the weight lifting off their shoulders and a peace overcomes them. Juntor even smiles and Quynn, in his barely conscious state, begins to mumble.

For a moment, as if in a trance, all the boys stand with peace on their faces and their eyes closed.

Then the first voice speaks and says, "now open your eyes young men, for you are in Aragopia."

The boys open their eyes one by one. Quynn sits up and stretches and yawns, as if waking from a deep sleep. Suddenly there is sound. Birds chirping, water running and the distant rumble of a waterfall transform the silence. The fog is gone and the sun shines brightly over a land more beautiful than any story ever told of such a place. The boys stand in awe, soaking up all that is to be seen, though it seems it may take a lifetime to accomplish.

"Welcome to Aragopia," says the first voice.

The boys look to the sources of the two voices. The first voice is that of a man-like creature, but with a peace in his being that separates him from regular men. His name is Nostradan. He is a Legna and a survivor of the wars with the Zirca lords. The other voice, the gruff voice is that of a giraffe. Long legs and a long neck covered by spots just like the ones the boys had seen near the Chimihog's compound. His name is Hermak.

"I have seen creatures like you, but I did not know your kind could talk," says Juntor.

"One of the many amazing things about Aragopia," says Nostradan. "His kind cannot talk, except for when in Aragopia. All forms of communication can be understood here."

"And you, you look like a man, but I have heard stories that describe your kind I believe. You are a Legna," says Senokre.

"That is correct," says Nostradan.

Nostradan's attention is drawn beyond the boys. The boys turn to see what he sees. A good ways off, Quynn stands holding a butterfly, his injury is healed and he is fully conscious. Though they cannot see, there are tears in his eyes as he looks upon the great landscape that makes Aragopia.

"Quynn," shouts Senokre. "You are better."

The boys run over to Quynn and look him over.

"Your leg, the bite, it's completely healed. There is no sign of any damage," says Juntor.

Senokre turns to Nostradan and Hermak and asks, "What did you do to fix his leg?"

"It is not what we did. This is Aragopia, there is no suffering here. This place has a strange effect on people," says Hermak.

The boys look at each other, still in a bit of shock of all that has happened in just a moment.

"We made it," says Quynn. "The old man was right and we made it."

The horizon is filled with the beauty of Aragopia, as far as the eye can see. There are mountains in the distance like a great wall marking the farthest corner of the land. In between are lakes glistening in the sunlight. Rivers run through the green terrain like tassel on a Christmas tree. Everything seems at peace and harmony.

The boys smile and laugh, and for a moment are children again laughing and giggling and roughhousing like boys do. Their two hosts stand back and watch them and all their excitement.

"It has been a long time since we've had new visitors. I have missed watching the joy and excitement of such a discovery as Aragopia," says Nostradan.

"They must be a special kind of human. To be so young and to brave such dangerous lands as they have to get here. A special breed they must be," says Hermak.

"When shall we tell them that there is so much more to discover here?" asks Nostradan.

"We have plenty of time," says Hermak. "Look at them, the joy of youth. Nothing is as fulfilling as the elation that shows in happy children's faces."

After watching for a few minutes, Hermak speaks up and says, "Well, there is much to see and I do not know how much time you plan to stay, but I am sure young ones have parents and parents worry when their children are missing, so let us continue your journey, for Aragopia is a large place and you have only just scratched the surface of this amazing land."

The boys acknowledge Hermak and go in the direction he points them. They walk with their hosts for a little distance until they meet up with another giraffe.

"This is Iras. He will be your guide," says Hermak.

Juntor looks at Hermak and Nostradan curiously. "You are leaving us now?"

"Yes," says Nostradan, "we have to tend to the boundaries of Aragopia and welcome new visitors that may get lost in the haze. But Iras is very knowledgeable of Aragopia and can tell you far more than either of us could."

"Farewell young humans," says Hermak.

The two walk away and the boys wave goodbye and watch their new acquaintances depart.

"I am Iras. I will be your guide through Aragopia. Are you ready?"

Without an answer, Iras begins to walk away. After a moment, the boys realize they might be left behind and all run to catch up with their new guide.

The group walks for a few hours. All along Iras points to interesting things and tells them a story about it. They see meadows of flowers and flowing grass, with all kinds of insects going about their business. Even the annoying bugs aren't so bad here in Aragopia.

A bee flies unnoticed by the crew and carefully lands on Quynn's arm.

"Oh, oh Quynn, there is a bee on your arm. Careful he doesn't sting you," says Juntor.

Quynn nervously looks at the bee on his arm, but he does not swat it. He studies it as it seems to study his arm for a moment.

"It will not sting you, young man," says Iras. "No need to kill it. Here in Aragopia, all evil is dissolved and no one thing will hurt another."

After a moment the bee takes to flight and goes about its daily business and the boys watch it then Quynn says, "You are right, it did not intend to harm me. But as I saw it I did not desire to kill it, either."

Before the boys can react to that moment, they walk upon a stream that has crept up to run alongside their path. The trickling of the water splashing against rocks and other obstacles creates a soothing sound. Juntor catches a glimpse of something in the water and pauses.

"Careful, I believe I saw an Albinogator in the stream," he says.

The boys stop and stare for a moment, though fear does not overcome them. Iras laughs a bold and hardy laugh.

"As I said, all things in Aragopia are good. No matter what threat they were in the outside world, here they have no desires for evil," says Iras then he asks, "You have had a run in with an Albinogator before?"

"Not an Albinogator, but like twenty or thirty," says Juntor.

Iras is amazed by the statement.

"He does not exaggerate. We ran into a pack of them when crossing the river just before we entered Aragopia," says Senokre.

"Hmm, that is very interesting in two ways," says Iras.

"How's that?" asks Quynn.

"Well one way that is interesting is the fact that you had a run in with those creatures and survived. Many sad stories have come from the outside over the years of men running into only a few Albinogators and seeing their very end," Iras says pausing to think.

"What about the other reason?" asks Quynn.

"I am surprised at there being so many this far, west. Hmm, it is as if something has stirred them. Nevertheless, let us move on," says Iras.

The journey continues on. The boys follow Iras northwest through the center of Aragopia. The aroma in the air is fresh, scented by the abundance of flowers spread along their journey.

"I have never really noticed flowers, but these are enchanting," says Senokre.

"He wishes he had a girlfriend back home that he could take some to," says Quynn.

The boys laugh with Senokre blushing a bit and they move on.

Further along, they here a call, like a horn of some valiant army of legend's past, ring through the lands. They look to find the source of the sound and see a large party of Legnas marching, as if to battle if not for the peace that covers this land.

"Those are Legnas, young men. You have already met one in Nostradan. They are the greatest creation of Kron. They were created for the battles with the evil Alohessy and his evil minions," says Iras.

They all watch the glory and magnificence that is the march of the Legnas. In perfect unison they march along, carrying long spears and wearing the traditional white robes with gold tassel. The group glows as the sun reflects off of their clothing creating the image of sacred beings. Only a few living humans have ever seen such an event.

"Where do they march to?" asks Juntor.

"They roam these lands waiting for 'the call'," says Iras.

"What is 'the call'?" asks Juntor.

"There are many, many things in this world that are not necessary to be known by such young ears. There is much I will show you and tell you, but there is not enough time to tell you all that there is. Besides, young men must be hungry. The sun is sinking away and night approaches. We must reach our resting spot soon. You need your rest. We have a long day of exploration that awaits us tomorrow," says Iras.

The expedition carries on into the twilight where they reach a small camp of several huts in a circle. A fire burns in the middle and light shines from inside a few of the buildings. As the boys get closer they see what appears to be human families preparing for a feast. The smell of cooked meat and vegetables, like a buffet, fills the air.

"Those are humans," says Senokre.

"Is there a big event happening, for they seem to be getting ready for a party?" asks Quynn.

"Word travels fast here. They set this feast for you," says Iras.

The boys walk into the camp and are greeted by several humble and smiling humans. Iras steps to the side and converses with a Legna called Gyran, who stands as a sentinel at the edge of the camp.

A lady, Sarah, shows the boys to their seats and directs two other young women to take their things for them. Sarah has a motherly spirit about her and her aura helps all who come into contact with her feel at home. The boys sit at the large table positioned in the center of the camp. The light of the fire brightens the table as strongly as if the sun itself was shining down on the feast. A young boy and a woman bring out some food and serve the boys.

"Welcome to Aragopia, young men. I am Sarah," says the kind lady.

The boys smile and speak to Sarah, but their stomachs overtake their manners, and with their noses urging them on, they dig into the meat and potatoes and fruits that cram the table.

Senokre manages to speak in between mouthfuls as he catches his breath and says, "This is a very delicious meal."

The other boys nod and continue filling themselves. The people of Aragopia, present at the party, partake and enjoy the meal as well. Even Iras and Gyran stuff their mouths with fruits. Giraffes don't eat meat and Legnas are vegetarians.

It is getting late now. The moon shines above and the stars twinkle on the black background that is the sky. The boys sit around the campfire, on a couple of old logs, with Iras, Gyran and a few humans, talking and asking questions.

"Thank you Sarah, for your hospitality," says Quynn. "You remind me of my mother. She used to cook big meals all the time. I do miss her."

"I am sure she misses you. You must have been away from home for a long time now," says Sarah.

Quynn looks at Sarah and smiles as tears come to his eyes. After a moment, he lowers his head. Sarah looks to Senokre.

"His mother died a while back," says Senokre.

"It is OK, Sarah. I just haven't thought of her in a long time, and you remind me so much of her," says a tearful Quynn.

Sarah smiles at Quynn and walks over to sit with him. She puts her arm around him and he lays his head on her shoulder. A very different Quynn than the boys are familiar with, sits vulnerable. This is the first time the boys had ever seen Quynn in this state.

"I know it will be," says Quynn.

"Where does the meat come from?" asks Juntor with a question from out of nowhere.

Iras laughs and answers, "A very good question Juntor.

We have hunters that go outside of the boundaries to hunt for food. It is impossible to kill living creatures here in Aragopia. A man has no desire to kill here, even for food."

"Do you know of Ranishi?" asks Senokre.

Iras looks at Senokre with surprise. Senokre feels his face flush, thinking he has embarrassed himself by bringing up a mythical children's hero.

Iras laughs and is joined by Gyran.

"Do I know of Ranishi? Who doesn't know of Ranishi? The greatest warrior in the greatest war, of course I know who Ranishi is," says Iras.

"Then the stories are true? He is the one who killed Alohessy and ended the war between humans and the Zirca lords? The one who never died and rides into battles when all is lost, wearing a green sheath on his left arm," says Senokre.

"All of the stories are true," says Iras.

"Does he live in Aragopia?" asks Juntor.

"He lives here, though he comes and goes, always on the move," says Iras.

"Where does he go?" asks Senokre.

Iras sighs and says, "Your questions always seem to lead back to the same topic. I will just tell you that he searches for Kron and that is all I will go into as far as that information goes and it is getting late, we must get to bed."

"Satisfy the boys' curiosity, Iras. It may be good for them to know all that they can since they could be the answer to all the prophesied events to come," says Gyran with a big smile on his face.

"Prophesied events, what events do you speak of?" asks Senokre.

"Gyran, you are no help. If you desire to tell the boys

all that there is to be known then you do so. Of course I believe you already have a mission at hand," says Iras, clearly annoyed by Gyran's efforts.

"If I did not have prior responsibilities, I would tell you young men all that there is to tell. But I must make my leave soon and will leave it to Iras to satisfy your interests," the Legna says.

The boys are confused, but realize not to ask anymore on the subject because they will get no answer tonight. They all go into a hut set just for them, settle in and quickly fall asleep.

Chapter 12

Zerin wakes early in the morning and walks outside of the small hut where he slept. A mist hovers above, trapped by the walls of the gorge that protect the village. Zerin inhales the fresh mountain air and stretches a bit.

The village is just waking and some of the villagers begin going about their usual business. Zerin looks over the secret community one more time, for some more memories to tell his friends then looks in the direction of the outlet to the mountain path and takes a deep breath. He does not know what the day will bring. Is his friend still alive? Will he run into a Fikron before he finds Lach? Can he survive an attack by the legendary creature? What if there is more than one?

Zerin speaks to himself, "I am an Arizz warrior. Fear is only to make me fight wiser, not to deter me from my mission."

"That is a wise saying, young Zerin. Where do you learn this from?" asks Mareege, who has walked up to Zerin.

"It just came to me as I felt fear begin to cause me to doubt myself," answers Zerin.

Mareege looks at Zerin with great amazement.

"If you would do an old man a favor, I wish to speak with you for a while. I would like to share with you some things that may help you on this journey, and maybe others," says Mareege.

Zerin thinks for a moment, at first feeling uninterested but seeing the determination in the old man's eyes, he agrees and walks with Mareege.

The conversation carries on as they walk around the small village and continues on as they arrive at the bamboo structure at the village center where they sit. The conversation lasts throughout the morning as the sun rises and the mist disappears.

As midday day begins, their conversation comes to an end. Zerin and the old man say goodbye and Zerin walks away toward the opening in the mountainside. Mareege watches his exit, still uncertain of what it is that he sees in Zerin. He looks at another old man that stands close by.

"I can't figure out what it is, but for a man as old as myself to be impressed with a boy that young, tells me there is something special in that youth," he says as he turns to go back to his normal routines.

"Will you come back and see us?" asks Yatique who has followed Zerin out to the edge of the village.

"I do not know. I shall try to one day, but it may be a long time away. I shall try, though," answers Zerin.

Zerin looks toward the village one last time and a shimmer from high up on the mountain side, above the village on a ledge, catches his eye. He stares at it for a moment. It gives him a feeling of hope, as if the mountain is winking at him to say it approves of the young warrior.

"What is that, that shines up on the mountain?" he asks Yatique.

"I do not know what it is, but every day when the sun is the highest, something on the mountain glimmers, like a symbol or something, but I do not know what it means," answers Yatique. "I have heard the elders say it is a sign to let us know that hope is always with us."

Zerin nods and after a few moments he looks down at Yatique and says, "Till we meet again."

Zerin show Yatique the Arizz way of saying hello and goodbye and bumps forearms with the young boy, then walks back on his path to find Lach. Yatique watches with all the admiration that a six year old would have of a twelve year old like Zerin who carries himself like a great warrior, something that a child like Yatique aspires to be.

The sun is still high in the sky, though it has taken its downward turn, showing the world that it is mid afternoon. Zerin has stopped his forward movement and searches carefully along the edge of the canyon.

The old man had told Zerin of an opening that would allow him to get back down into the canyon bottom, a place that would be close to the Fikron den. The old man also told Zerin a possible strategy for freeing Lach, just in case Lach had been captured and imprisoned by the Fikron King. Now Zerin is in the area where this path to the bottom is supposed to be and he searches desperately to find it. He wants to get as far as possible before nightfall.

Zerin's eyes light up. He spots a slight opening at the edge of the canyon. It isn't much, but it is a better option than any other for getting down the steep wall. He takes a deep breath and begins to climb down.

The journey down is much easier than the climb up that he endured yesterday, and he reaches the area of the wall with all the caves and paths that zigzag along the canyon's edge all the way to the bottom. He gazes about the canyon and recognizes some of the landmarks from the first time he traveled through. The cave opening that leads to the Fikron den is now just a few hundred feet away.

Where is Lach? For sure he is somewhere in the vicinity of this dangerous area because there is no way Lach would be deterred from his chosen mission.

Zerin walks along the bottom edge of the canyon wall, using it for some level of stealth. The cave system that surrounds the Fikron den is like a maze, but Zerin thinks that if he can get back to the cave near that creature, Wilber, he can navigate his way to the den. This seems like a good start. At this point, if his friend is dead, surely remnants of him will be stored in the den. If Lach has already conquered the evil creatures, then he will probably still be in the den, reveling in his glory. So this is the strategy that Zerin chooses.

Desiring to avoid as much trouble as possible, Zerin chooses to work his way to the center of the canyon. He then uses the dry river bed to travel up the canyon. As with before, when he and his friends had walked down the canyon, the natural path provides some level of protection with the occasional tree and small bush that dot its edges.

After a small walk, Zerin spots the cave that his party had entered so many days ago. He squats by a bush and looks across the canyon floor. With no sign of trouble, he hustles in a bent over jog, toward the cave opening.

A hint of an odor floats in the air. Zerin shakes his head, knowing the smell is that of Wilber. With one more glance around, Zerin enters the cave.

After a moment his eyes adapt to the darkness and he sees the cave split into two. He takes the smaller opening and feels his way along the wall, searching for the small opening that leads to the Fikron den. The smell of Wilber increases, the closer Zerin gets to the gross being's chamber.

"Found it," says Zerin as he finds the opening, and darts in.

Zerin moves carefully through the small passage. He is unsure of where the drop off is. Since the boys had rushed down this corridor and with all the commotion, he was unsure of exactly how far down the invisible hole waited.

A feint noise carries through the cave, giving a much needed radar, since the noises come from the very hole that Zerin seeks. He arrives at the hole and listens. The noises are that of voices, like arguing. As he listens, he recognizes the defiant speech.

"Lach," he says in an excited whisper.

Zerin's first instinct is to jump down the hole and rush to his friend's side. It is obvious, from what Zerin can hear, that Lach is in some sort of trouble. Zerin pauses though, for there are no sounds of fighting.

He wants to get a better look so he decides to sneak up

on the Fikron den to evaluate the situation. A little experience goes a long way and Zerin wisely ties a bit of rope which he has carried in his bag to a jagged stone at the edge of the hole. This will provide a way back out, since going out through the Fikron den will probably not be possible, as it had been the first time he ventured through this place.

He climbs down the rocky slide and cringes, as once again, he feels the crackling of skeleton bones under his feet. He follows the light and the noise to the opening to the Fikron den and looks inside.

Inside, shouting at the top of his lungs, is Lach. As enraged as Zerin has ever seen him, Lach stands at the side of the den shouting challenges toward the center of the room.

There sits a jet black creature, scarier than any other creature in all the land, a killing machine, a perfect combination of lean muscles, huge fangs, and eyes that could scare a man to his death without touching him and black fur so dark that it seems to suck in the light around it. It is the Fikron King, which sits upon its throne, observing Lach's defiance. A few other Fikrons lie around in their grass beds, some gnawing on bones and watching the fearless young human.

Lach is bloody and battered, showing he put up a violent fight before being captured. A chain clings to his leg. His ankle is red and blistered from where he has lunged and pulled against his binds, trying desperately to attack his foe.

"You fear me. This is why you chain me to a wall. I challenge you, oh great king. I am just a boy. I am no threat to your mighty power. Release me and accept my challenge," Lach shouts with a raspy voice, having strained his vocal chords from hours of ranting.

Zerin watches further, trying to read the Fikron's intentions and looking over Lach's condition. His train of thought is broken when he hears the Fikron King speak.

"Shut your mouth, little man. Your voice has begun to sting my ears like the smelly man's stench stings my nose," says the master of the Fikrons.

"Shut it for me, o brave creature of the night," shouts back Lach, never short of defiant words.

The Fikron King snarls in a Fikron language that draws some animalistic laughter from the other Fikrons that line the den.

From Zerin's vantage point, he can only see the back of Lach, so he is unable to let his friend know that help has arrived. A rage begins to grow in Zerin as he looks at his bruised and battered friend. Zerin grips his sword and prepares for an attack. He will rescue his friend or he will die by his side.

His rage is interrupted by an attack of logic and he asks himself, "Why has the Fikron King not killed Lach? Why does he keep him alive?"

Zerin collects his thoughts and takes the moment to devise a strategy, calling on some of Mareege's words of using intelligence over brute force. Perhaps his original plan, and probably that of Lach's as well, to assault the Fikron den head on was not such a good idea.

Zerin rushes back to his rope, climbs out of the Fikron trash pit and rushes down the small cave.

In the Fikron den, Lach continues his verbal onslaught. A Fikron, who has apparently become tired of the loud boy, has slipped up close to Lach. Lach does not see the cat-like creature behind him and continues to challenge the Fikron

King. The Fikron King, who had momentarily looked down to chew on a bone, looks up and snarls at the agitated Fikron. Lach looks back to see the Fikron's razor sharp claws fully extended and its paw set for a strike, a strike that would surely have separated the young warrior from his head. The Fikron backs away as commanded by his king, but before it can settle back into its grass bed, Lach shouts challenges at it.

"Be careful what you wish for boy," says the Fikron King. "If I did not think you are of the bloodline of Gokar, I would make you a toy for my soldiers. Then you could spend the rest of you short life, not shouting words of challenge, but screaming words, begging for your life. A slow and tortuous death would be all that you are remembered for."

Sometime later Lach has lessened his shouts, but he stares, unwavering, at the Fikron King. Many of the Fikron soldiers sleep, having been given some relief from the noisy onslaught.

The atmosphere changes as a clatter comes from the skeleton room. The Fikron King gives an aware Fikron a nod to check on the noise, but before the Fikron can get to the opening a familiar voice carries into the den, followed by an all too familiar odor.

The Fikron King snarls to the other Fikrons in their language that translates into two words, "Smelly man."

The Fikrons get up, some slowly as they wake from their afternoon naps, and exit the den. The Fikron King smirks at Lach and follows suit.

Lach's nostrils burn and he knows who it is before it exits the skeleton room into the den. It is Wilber. The deformed man walks in and looks around.

"He is here and they have left. I told you, they fear me," Wilber says toward someone in the skeleton room.

This is not an unusual occasion. Every once in a while, a clumsy Wilber will stumble down the hole falling into the skeleton room and the Fikrons, not being able to stomach the odor, just exit the caves and wait until Wilber works his way out, exits the cave and the smell clears.

The smell of the creature was too much even to kill, as it would leave a taste in their mouths so awful that they would not be able to keep food down. The taste would stay in their mouths so long, that they would starve to death.

Lach looks to see who it is that Wilber talks to and out steps Zerin, sword drawn. He walks over to Lach and chops at the chain, wasting no time, being uncertain of how long the Fikron will stay out. A few chops are all it takes to break the rusty chain and Lach is freed.

They greet each other quickly and Zerin turns to go back into the skeleton room. Lach doesn't follow immediately and goes to the throne and grabs the medallion that had been taken from him soon after his capture. He then follows Zerin.

"Stay in here for a few minutes, then leave the cave, like you normally do," Zerin says to Wilber.

"Oh, I will stay for a little. I like to look around. The Fikrons always have good stuff to plunder through," says Wilber.

Zerin and Lach nod and exit the den, hurrying through the skeleton room, climbing the rope and racing toward their cave exit.

As the boys reach the cave opening, they slow and carefully peer outside into the canyon. They both scan the terrain and hurry out of the cave, down the small path to the nearest bush. There they squat and take a moment to catch their breath.

"Are you alright?" asks Zerin, eyeing Lach's injuries.

"I am fine," answers Lach.

"We should rest only for a moment. Once those creatures discover you are gone, they will be hunting us. We should get as far of a head start as we can. They know this terrain much better than we do," says Zerin.

"I am not leaving. I am not finished here," says Lach.

"Lach, we are outnumbered. They did not kill you before, but that does not mean they will not kill you this time around," says Zerin.

"I cannot leave that creature to live. It has dishonored Olkar's bloodline and though I am not blood related, I carry the honor of his family on my shoulders," says Lach.

"We cannot stay here. We must get out of these dangerous lands and get back home," says Zerin.

"I will not leave that devil to live in peace. I must kill it, Zerin. It is my destiny," says Lach.

"Lach, perhaps it is your destiny, but not now. We must leave here. We have to check on our friends as well. I left them two days walk back and they were going to continue on toward Aragopia. If they have gotten into trouble, we need to get to them as soon as possible. We may be their only hope," says Zerin.

Lach takes a heavy breath and accepts Zerin's words. One thing that could equal Lach's thirst for vengeance was his protective nature over those he perceived as weaker than he. So he submits to Zerin's will and the two boys prepare to leave.

They run across to the dry river bed and follow its path. As they pass by the cave leading to the Fikron den, they see the Fikrons still lounging around the outside, still waiting for Wilber to exit.

The boys jog throughout the rest of the day until the light disappears and they can see no more. The exhausted duo forego setting up camp and just find a comfortable spot underneath a large tree surrounded by a few bushes. Hoping that the brush was enough to hide them from detection, they uneasily fall asleep.

Chapter 13

A rooster crows in the distance, letting everyone know of the new day's arrival. The boys get up, yawn and stretch. This being the first real good night's sleep they've had since leaving home, they feel new and refreshed. They get ready and gather their things. Quynn talks with Sarah over to the side, while the other boys wait for Iras.

"Let's move along young men. We have much more to see," says Iras who approaches from behind.

Iras leads and the boys follow. Their path still heads northwest, toward the center of Aragopia.

The boys walk along talking and enjoying the consistently beautiful landscape. The path has turned southward now, but the terrain is no less beautiful than before. Always there is a brook close by playing its delightful tune. The trees that stand here and there along the path shudder in the light breeze. The sounds mix with the sounds of birds going about their daily chores singing their special songs.

The tranquility is brought to an abrupt stop when an image of a creature, as black as night, crosses their path up ahead and then out of sight into the heavy brush beside the road. The boys stop.

"What is it?" asks Iras.

The boys stare at the area where they thought they had seen something, but after a few minutes feel their eyes have betrayed them and they continue on. Suddenly a rustling in the brushy area beside their path catches their attention.

"What is that Iras?" asks Juntor.

The boys stare into the brush trying to draw a mark on what is causing the rustling. Something catches Brenka-uku's sight. Something has stepped onto the path ahead.

"Fikron," says Brenka-uku cautiously.

The boys look to see a Fikron standing on the path, not twenty yards away, staring at them. They look to Iras, who stands, studying the Fikron.

"Iras?" asks Juntor.

Iras stands silent. The stare down between the Fikron and the group continues for a moment. The creature stares at all the boys glaringly and doesn't blink, even once. The boys look to Iras then back at the black creature. The tense moment is broken up when the Fikron speaks.

"Long time no see old buddy," says the Fikron. "Don't just stand there looking at me like I am 'The One'."

Iras smiles and breathes a sigh of relief.

"Arak, you prankster," says Iras.

Iras walks over to Arak, leaving the boys standing a bit stunned.

"What just happened?" asks Quynn.

"I do not know. I was kind of scared, but I could not pull my sword," says Senokre.

Still a little confused, Juntor asks, "So it is not a bad Fikron?

The boys see Arak and Iras laughing and talking like two longtime friends.

"I guess not," says Senokre.

Iras signals the boys to come over and meet Arak. They do, feeling more curious than cautious.

"This is Arak," says Iras.

"And yes, I am a Fikron," says the jet black creature.

The boys stand silent, studying this rare creature that only a few have seen and most have never survived to tell about. Now it stands in front of them with all the magnificent features of the evil Fikron. The perfect killing machine and the definition of evil stands in front of them laughing and joking.

"I take it I am not the first Fikron you have encountered, but I assure you that I have repented of my evil ways. This Aragopia makes it impossible for anything to be evil when inside its boundaries...," Arak says and then with a pause he says, "...except of course, 'The One'."

The boys' eyes light up with interest. Iras shakes his head and says, "Well Arak, it has come to my attention that these young men are very curious about the things I would rather not tell them. But you seem to be of no help, so let us all sit and I will tell you boys this story that seems to have snuck its way into you curiosities."

The boys all sit around and Iras begins the story and says, "There is a prophecy that a great battle is to come. Not a battle between groups of people for a territory or some riches, but a battle for existence.

An evil is to arise. A creature so evil, that even the powers of Aragopia will have no influence on its soul."

"Many believe the Fikron King is that evil, and that is why he avoids even getting close to the boundaries of Aragopia, for he has yet to master all the evil potential he has. He waits for the moment when he is ready, whether it is tomorrow or hundreds of years from now. Because you see, Fikrons live forever, even without Aragopia's anti-aging powers," says Arak.

"Well yes," says Iras, "many believe that the Fikron King is that evil creature, but some say 'The One' has yet to be born, that the demon seed lurks, waiting to take the body of whomever it desires for its evil deeds."

"Ah, there is no evil greater than that of the Fikron King," says Arak.

Iras submits to Arak's unrelenting opinion and continues the story. "So this is why the Legnas wait and why Ranishi sets out in search of Kron. You see, this evil will enter the land of Aragopia and it will not be swayed by the goodness here. It will not reveal its bad intentions and will go to the very gates of Brigal's realm. It will seek council with the Zirca lord and from there it will tempt him with offers and promises," says Iras.

"I thought that Brigal repented of his ways and that is why he created Aragopia?" asks Senokre.

"Very true, Senokre, and I do not pretend to know how or why, but the prophecy states this will happen," says Iras.

Well, then Ranishi can just kill Brigal like he did Alohessy," says Quynn.

"But Ranishi did not kill Alohessy by his bare hands. He had to use Alohessy's very own sword, created for the sole purpose of killing the god Kron. But the sword was lost," says Iras.

"Lost?" asks Brenka-uku.

"Yes. Ranishi did not leave his battle with Alohessy unscathed. He was badly injured and after he killed Alohessy on the side of the mountain, he struggled to get back to his people, but he passed out and a rogue group of mountain people found him and cared for him, until he was well enough to travel and return to his home.

The sword was either lost or it was left with those people. But no one knows who they are or where they live. Ranishi was in too bad of shape to remember how he got there," says Iras.

"Then how can anyone possibly kill Brigal. He has almost as much power as Alohessy. Surely he cannot be killed any other way?" ask Senokre.

Smiling, Arak says, "There is one way."

"How?" asks Juntor.

"Why the one who creates something, can also destroy it," says Iras.

The boys ponder the riddle for a moment and Juntor excitedly yells out his answer, "Kron!"

"Very good young fellow," says Iras.

"But we have to find Kron and no one has seen him since the Great War," says Arak.

"Where is he?" asks Quynn.

"After Alohessy and his army defeated the Legnas, he and Brigal tricked Kron into going into the mountains, into a series of caves that are a maze under the Pryon Mountains. Kron went in believing his favorite creation, Dorisha, was being held captive and now he cannot find his way out. Kron needs to be found, so that there will be an answer to Brigal's impending onslaught," says Iras.

Senokre glances at Quynn then asks, "Is it possible that Kron has escaped the caves?"

"If he has escaped then he would have revealed himself and taken his thrown over all Thrae," says Iras.

"It's just that we met a man on our journey, by the name of Nork. He said many things that only someone like Kron would know," says Senokre.

"You say a man? What did he look like?" asks Iras.

"I would say he was not too old in appearance and somewhat gangly, but very wise. He lives with Brenka-uku's tribe."

Iras muses over Senokre's words for a moment and then says, "No, this cannot be Kron, for Kron is god over this world and in no way would he be anything less than glorious and powerful in his appearance."

"What do you think, Brenka?" asks Senokre.

"I have known him all of my life, and though he is very mysterious, I do not believe he is anything more than a paranoid, but wise and experienced man," Brenka-uku answers.

Senokre's shoulders slump as he accepts defeat in the debate.

"But nevertheless, we shall continue to search for him

and prepare for this war of wars that is to come," says Iras.

Iras looks up into the sky at the sun, which tells that it is late afternoon now and they must get moving along. The boys say goodbye to Arak and follow their guide, continuing along their path.

The group comes upon a plateau. It is small in size but rises about a hundred feet, like a natural watchtower. A path leads around the edge to the top. Iras admires the landmark and turns to the boys.

"Ah, this I must show you. This is called the Table of Kron. It gets its name because at the top, you can see over all of Aragopia and beyond. It is said Kron would sit upon the Table and look over his creations. We will go to the top. It will not take long and if there is only one memory of Aragopia that you take back, it should be from the top," says Iras.

The boys follow Iras up the spiraling path. It is just wide enough for them to walk single file. The surface of the path is very rocky and the boys slip and stumble along and begin to wonder if this much effort will be worth whatever reward waits at the top.

Finally they reach the top and huff and puff to catch their breath, with their hands on their knees looking at the ground.

"Look up, look around and see the majesty of Aragopia," demands Iras.

The terrain along the boys' journey had risen in elevation and now on top of the raised patch of land that Iras refers to as the Table, the boys can see over all of Aragopia. From the snowcapped mountains in the far northwest corner where Brigal lives in seclusion to the east corner where the boys first entered the mystical land, all of the beauty presents itself, like a large painting created by the greatest painter. They look over the great land, realizing this may be the last time they ever see such a sight.

Drumbeats in the distance pull the boys out of their trance. Iras stares long and hard toward the noise. The boys follow suit. They see in the far distance what appears to be a gathering of sorts.

Suddenly Iras' eyes brighten up. He hurries over to a wooden item standing upright along the edge of the plateau It has a glass-like, clear, flat stone on top of it. He swivels it around and looks through the transparent stone toward the noise and smiles.

"Come, look through this," says Iras.

Senokre is first and he looks into the strange item.

"There, focus there," says Iras pointing Senokre in the right direction. "What do you see?"

Senokre stares for a moment, blinks a little as he struggles to focus in on the commotion.

"I see something like a parade. There are people gathered and a group, on horses, rides through them. The people seem to be cheering the men on horseback."

"What about the one leading the men on horseback? Describe him," says Iras.

Senokre swallows hard, his jaw drops open then he says, "He wears a green sheath on his left arm."

Senokre looks at Iras and asks, "It is Ranishi?"

Iras nods his head as the other boys race to the magnifying object and wrestle for their chance to look upon the greatest warrior the world has ever known.

Iras smiles and laughs as the boys all get their turn to

see Ranishi. After they are done, they smile, no longer questioning their journey to the top. They talk amongst themselves for a bit, reveling in what they have seen.

Senokre says, "I wish Lach was here to see this."

Juntor laughs and says, "maybe not, for he may have challenged him for the right to be known as the greatest warrior."

The other boys laugh and they continue to joke around and talk about things that boys their age find interesting.

A little while later, while the boys are all sitting around a circle with Iras still joking and laughing and talking, a Legna walks up.

Iras greets him. "Welcome Surl. How might you be this fine day?"

"I am well Iras," says Surl.

Iras looks at the boys and says, "There is one other thing I wish to show you."

Iras calls the boys over to the opposite side of the plateau and points.

"That is the edge of Aragopia. Your journey is complete. It is time for you to go home now. You are brave young warriors and you have accomplished something that very few have ever done. You came in search of a mythical land and you have found it and experienced it. You will forever benefit in your lives from this event and I see that you all will be leaders of your people one day, but for now, you are still children and children must return to their families, until the day comes when they are old enough to go out on their own for good," says Iras.

The boys look and they see the clearly marked boundary of trees and rock. They realize that Iras is right and though they hate to leave, they also are ready to get back to their normal lives and to tell all that will listen about their adventure.

"Surl will be your guide. He is going to lead you a different way out toward you lands. There is word that the Fikrons are stirring, as if hunting for something, and it is no longer safe to take the same route back," says Iras.

"We were hoping to find our friends on the way back," says Senokre.

"It is too dangerous. Gyran, the Legna you met at the feast, has gone in search of your friends. He and another have gone by horseback and they are fast riders. I hope they can find your friends in time," says Iras.

"There is nothing that can be done for your part. You just have to hope for the best that no harm has come to your friends before they are found by Gyran. But I do not recommend you going that way. There are Fikrons roaming those lands in ways that haven't been seen since the early days of this world," says Surl.

"He is right. Our best bet is to get home and arrange a group to go and find them, but knowing Lach and Zerin, it will not surprise me if they are just fine. After all, they are Lach and Zerin," says Senokre.

"Good. We will camp here tonight, and tomorrow you will begin your journey home," says Iras.

It is full dark now. A fire lights the boys' camp where they sit around and talk. Iras and Surl sit with them, enjoying their stories and answering the occasional question to the best of their ability.

"Can you tell us a little more about Fikrons?" asks

Juntor.

"Fikrons were created for one reason, to fight Kron, which is where they get their name. Their sole mission is to find Kron and destroy him," says Iras.

"But can they kill Kron? I would think Kron would be too strong to be killed by Fikron," says Senokre.

"You are correct, except it is unknown about the Fikron king. It is assumed that Kron cannot be killed. But Kron himself was surprised at the power of his first creation, and it raises many questions concerning whether or not Alohessy could create a creature powerful enough to pull off this deed. The Fikron king has unusual powers compared to the rest. He can speak and understand our language which is quiet impressive in itself. There are many questions about just what the king of the Fikrons is capable of," says Surl.

"Many believe the Fikron do not realize Alohessy is dead and that is why they continue their battle against humans and continue to search for Kron, so that Alohessy may kill him. You see, I believe Alohessy wished he never tricked Kron into going into the caves, and wished he had killed him instead," says Iras.

"I don't believe Kron can be killed, but I believe that Alohessy in his arrogance and jealousy believed he was capable of killing his creator," says Surl.

"But these are all stories and no one really knows for sure. All we can do is see how it all plays out in the end," says Iras.

"I heard that if a man killed a Fikron, that it would give him strange powers. Have you heard of this?" asks Senokre.

"I have not heard of this. If a man is able to kill a

Fikron, I believe he already possesses strange powers. Fikrons are the most dangerous creatures that exist," says Iras.

"I have heard of what you speak," says Surl. "I have heard that a man will possess some great strength, if he kills a Fikron. But, I have also heard that there are words, called Warrior Speak, that release this strength in times of great trouble."

"I have heard of Warrior Speak, but I have heard it will signal the leaders in the time of the war of wars that we discussed with Arak," says Iras.

"Who knows the Warrior Speak?" asks Juntor.

"They say some of the original humans who were involved in the Great War with Alohessy had killed Fikrons and knew the Warrior Speak. But they have been deceased a long time," says Surl.

"What about Ranishi?" asks Juntor.

"I do not know. I have never heard of any mention of it," says Iras.

"I'm afraid I do not know the answer to that either," says Surl.

"Well, when I get home, I'm going to learn all that there is to know about these myths and legends, because Aragopia was just a myth not too long ago, so I'll never say something does not exist," says an enthusiastic Juntor.

"Home, it was not just until you said that that I realized how much I do miss my home," says Senokre.

"Yeah, I do look forward to eating some of my grandmother's pies. Just thinking about it makes my stomach growl," says Juntor.

"I will have to delay my return home for a few weeks,

for I am most curious about your homes and your land and I plan to accompany you all the way," says Brenka-uku. "Though I will be excited to return home and tell them all that I have seen."

The boys continue talking about their memories of home and what they plan to do when they get back, all except Quynn, who is noticeably absent from the conversation. Iras recognizes this and speaks with Quynn off to the side.

After a while the moon peaks overhead as the campfire dwindles. All settle into the makeshift beds and stare at the stars, thinking. What a feat for these young men to have not only taken part in, but successfully completed. With all the obstacles, they had survived and learned to work together as a team, like Arizz warriors are supposed to.

A bright morning sky wakes the boys and they yawn and stretch before finally getting up and gathering their things. They all journey together down the thin, spiraling path that leads back down to the bottom. At the bottom a mix of excitement and dread overtake the boys, because for as excited as they are about going home, they know they have to say goodbye to Aragopia and their new friends.

Iras and Surl walk a small distance away from the boys and Quynn calls the boys to gather with him.

"Are we ready to head back home?" asks Senokre.

"There is something I need to tell you guys," says Quynn with a tear in his eye. He stutters in his speech and pauses for a moment, gathers himself and says, "I'm not going back."

The boys stare, shocked and confused.

"I didn't tell you before, but the whole reason I came

on this trip was because my father, he died. So now both my parents are dead and I have nothing to go back to. So I came on this journey searching for something else. What exactly I was searching for, I do not know. But I do know what I found," says Quynn.

"Aragopia," says a teary eyed Juntor, who lightheartedly punches Quynn shoulder.

"Yes, I, I mean we found this wonderful place. But I think what I found, that is even better than that, was that I have the greatest friends in all the lands and I will miss you all and I will never forget our journey together. Our good times and our bad..." Quynn and Juntor exchange smiles, "...will be the most wonderful time in my life which I will never forget."

One by one the boys hug Quynn and say goodbye, the last being Juntor. Quynn holds Juntor's arm before he can walk away.

"I just want to tell you, that I was hard on you and I wasn't fair. I was wrong about you and I know that you are and will become a great warrior. I tell you this also, because I know what you have to deal with when you are at home and I want you to know that it is not your fault. You are a better man than him. He treats you wrong, but I believe in all his faults, he loves you, because you are his only son. Do not hate your father, rise above and realize he needs you more than you need him," Quynn says.

Juntor fights back his tears, but is too choked up to respond and can only look at Quynn through watery eyes and nod. Not feeling his response is enough; he hugs Quynn one last time and walks away.

The boys join Surl. Iras and Quynn watch as they

walk away, further and further out of sight, toward their home as Quynn begins to embrace his new home.

The journey home with Surl goes smoothly. The land in the southeast is mostly absent of humans and most predators of man. The boys trek through a thin strip of trees that make up the border. They feel an immediate difference in comfort as they exit the lands of Aragopia. No more is the peace they had felt, but a sense of caution sets the mood.

They continue on and come upon a large field of fountains. There are fountains of all sizes. The waters vary from perfectly clear to differing colors and steam rises out of a few of the hotter ones. As they walk through the land of fountains, Surl tells them a little about its history.

"These are the Fountains of Talpri. First I will tell you, do not drink the water. There are many legends that go along with this land. I do not know if these stories are true or make believe, but they are interesting, nonetheless," says Surl.

The boys follow along and listen, all the while gazing at the unusual terrain.

"The legend I have heard the most is that some of the fountains have magic water, but some have poison. It is said that there is good magic and bad magic. I do not know what the good magic is and I do not want to know what the bad magic is. So it is just best to look and not touch," says Surl.

"Does anyone know which fountain has what in it?" asks Juntor.

"Well, you see, it is said that different beings have different reactions, so Brenka-uku may have a different reaction after drinking some of the water than you boys and I would respond differently than you as well.

As far as your question goes, I am not sure. It is said that the Zirca know, but their kind has long since been eliminated. So it seems that it may never be known. Even the animals do not drink from these fountains," says Surl.

"I know a man who claims to have seen a Fikron drinking from one of the fountains, long ago," says Senokre.

"If your friend is telling the truth then he is like you, one of the lucky few outside of Aragopia that has seen a Fikron and lived to tell about it. But I doubt the story, for I do not believe even the Fikron know which water is safe to drink," says Surl.

"So far, all that the man told us has been accurate, so I do not believe him to be lying," says Senokre.

"This is very odd. I have seen Fikrons around these fountains, but they never took a drink," says Surl. "This is something to consider because even though he is not known to journey this close to Aragopia, it has been said that the Fikron King may know which fountains are safe to drink from. This is very interesting and something I will have to report to Ranishi once I return."

The boys get a few last glimpses of the odd place and continue on their way, traveling on to flatter lands. As they get closer to the prairie lands which they are most familiar with, Surl begins to lead them in an easterly direction.

"I would show you the old lands of Miklidor and Suna-Nora, but it seems an evil has taken them over and I believe it would be easier to lead you to the original path that you traveled to get to Aragopia. That is where I will leave you," says Surl.

"You should join us to our lands and have a meal with

us," says Juntor.

"I am afraid that your people, those that know of us, harbor hard feelings. You see, it is believed by a lot of your ancestors that my kind abandoned them in the wars with Alohessy and most that know of our good deeds did not survive the war. So the bad stories have been passed along through history," says Surl.

"I have never heard of Legnas or anything bad about your kind," says Senokre.

"Only a few of your oldest still know, but it only takes the words of a trusted few to turn a group against a stranger," says Surl.

The boys accept and continue to follow Surl, talking and observing all the scenery throughout the day, while the sun is high and as the sun sets. As the afternoon comes to its end, the boys arrive at the area they are familiar with. In the vicinity of their original path, Surl pauses and turns toward the boys to say farewell.

"It was nice meeting you Surl and thank you for guiding us," says Senokre.

"It was an honor to meet such brave young men and I will tell many about you. Now I will tell you, to sleep cautious tonight because Fikrons have been seen in these lands. Most of the time it is rare to see them here, but it is always good to be on the safe side," says Surl.

The boys nod and Surl turns and begins his journey back to his home. The boys watch as he walks away, and realize at that moment that Surl may be the last remnant of Aragopia they will ever see.

After Surl is out of sight the boys decide to setup camp. It is almost dark now and they hope to make it home by tomorrow evening, so they go to sleep early so they may rise early and complete their journey. Though it is not easy for them to fall asleep, with their missing friends on their minds, they manage to do so. It has been a long day.

As the first sign of light moves over the land, the boys rise from their slumber. Excited and eager to return home, they pack up there things and joke and laugh together. As they begin to start the final leg of their journey home, Brenka-uku pauses and stares at something on the ground, just a short way from their camp. The other boys notice.

"Let's go Brenka. We haven't much further to go. What are you looking at?" asks Senokre.

"Look at this," says Brenka-uku.

The boys study what Brenka-uku has pointed out. It is some sort of footprint.

"What do you think it is?" asks Juntor.

"It looks like a paw print, like a large cat. It looks like a Fikron," says Brenka-uku.

The boys look around, searching the terrain for any sign of movement or hint of the evil that is a Fikron.

A rustle in a distant bush draws the eye of the Chimihog.

"There!" he exclaims.

Chapter 14

After surviving at least one more night Lach and Zerin are well on their way. It is about the middle of a hot day, and sweat pours from their pores. They cautiously walk along the dry riverbed, looking down at the sandy soil for tracks and then back up to gaze across the horizon for signs of danger. Their conversation is kept to a minimum. There will be time for sharing stories when they are in safer places. Every once in a while a hand comes up, signaling a stop. The boys scan the area where they may have seen something suspicious. Once it is considered safe, they continue on.

Their cautious advance carries on until dusk as they finally reach the end of the canyon. Being early evening, there is still plenty of light to travel a little further.

"Which way shall we go?" asks Lach.

"I am not sure. If we go right, toward Aragopia we may run into our friends. But, this is the third day since I left them. I do not know if they have continued looking for Aragopia or if they have turned back for home," says Zerin.

"I do not wish to abandon them to these lands. I would like to know what has happened to them," says Lach.

"I feel confident that they will not be captives of the Fikrons. I would think we would have seen Fikrons carrying captives back to their lair," says Zerin. "But as for their fate beyond that, I do not know."

The boys ponder their options. Torn between considering the worst and the best of their friend's situation, they find this to be one of the harder decisions they have had to make on this journey. Even young warriors desire the comforts of their homeland and even the most amazing adventures get old eventually.

A noise from just beyond a clump of trees releases them from their burden. As they listen more intently, they make out the noise to be some sort of fight, or the end of one judging by the groaning sound of one of the participants in the ruckus beyond the green and brown wall.

Lach and Zerin look at each other then race toward the action. There is no verbal communication between the two, but both carry the same concern, could this be their friends in trouble?

Lach and Zerin's rush to the chaos takes them past the body of a dead Legna. They slow their pace as they observe the unusual being, having never seen one before. The deceased Legna has been mauled quiet severely, but enough can be assessed to draw the conclusion that it is not human, though it has many human characteristics.

As they arrive on the scene, they see a fierce black creature swiping at another Legna, throwing the being high in the air and watching it crash to the earth with a thud. They see that the attacker is a Fikron which now watches its prey, waiting for something. The Legna is still alive and once he gains some energy, he tries to get up and escape, only to be met with another brutal swipe, knocking it high into the air and back down with a bone breaking thud.

The Fikron does not see the boys approach, but they watch it in horror as it seems to be playing with the dying Legna. As if enjoying the torture more than the kill, the Fikron is completely immersed in its playtime.

The boys yell at the top of their lungs, swords drawn as they run up on the Fikron. In its surprise, the Fikron is startled, and runs off and out of sight over a small hill. The boys run to the Legna and squat by its side.

"He's hurt real bad," says Zerin.

The Legna stares up at the boys out of one eye. The other eye is swollen shut. Claw marks cover his body and clothing. He struggles for breath as blood chokes him, causing him to have to spit what he can out onto the ground beside him. One of his legs is so mangled, it is impossible to tell which bend is that of his knee joint and that of bone snapped in two.

"Can you speak? What is your name?" asks Zerin.

Struggling to breathe, the Legna forces out his name, and says, "Gyran."

Gyran and the other Legna had ridden all through the night in search of Lach and Zerin. Ironically their mission was to find the boys before it was too late, which in this turn of events, has become the boys who have found the Legnas, but too late.

"Is there anything we can do for you?" asks Zerin.

"Your names?" asks Gyran, just as he chokes on some blood.

"I am Zerin and this is Lach."

The Legna forces a smile through his swollen, bloody lips and says, "I found you."

Zerin looks at him confused.

"Your friends are safe. They are headed for home," says Gyran, looking southward with his eye, "south, south of here."

"Our friends are OK? They are heading south?" asks Zerin.

The Legna forces a nod. Zerin nods back.

Lach interrupts the interaction and says," the Fikron is coming back. You stay here and I will go take care of it."

Busy trying to figure out what to do for the dying Legna, Zerin doesn't get a chance to stop Lach, who is now running full force in the direction of Gyran's killer.

"Wait here Gyran. I must help my friend kill this creature. I will be right back," says Zerin.

Zerin gets up and runs toward the noise that begins to carry from the other side of the hill. Lach has encountered the beast and their battle has begun.

Lach swings wildly at the Fikron. Showing the reflexes of a cat, the dark monster dodges Lach's attack, but not without struggle as it loses its footing and trips over a large rock. Having four legs comes in handy and the Fikron recovers quickly and moves back into the standoff with Lach. Lach lunges at the Fikron, attempting to stab the Fikron in the heart. The Fikron dodges and spins, causing Lach to lose his balance. It swipes at Lach, but is blocked by Lach's sword. The impact knocks the sword out of Lach's hand and it goes flying fifty feet away. The cat swipes at Lach's head, but Lach dodges and flips underneath a second swipe to wind up behind the Fikron. They face off again.

"Bring it, cowardly devil. I will fight you with no sword. I will separate your head from your body with my bare hands and personally carry it back to your poser king. Then I shall separate his," Lach says in typical Lach style.

The black cat and Lach circle. As the Fikron circles, he winds up with his back to a large boulder that sits to the side. Neither Lach, nor the Fikron see Zerin climbing to the top of the boulder. Zerin preps himself, his sword overhead, ready to strike.

At the last minute, Lach sees Zerin and shouts, "No!"

Zerin jumps from the rock platform and stabs the unsuspecting cat in the back. The blow does not kill the Fikron and it bucks around in pain with the sword still embedded in its flesh and Zerin holding on as if riding a mad bull at a rodeo.

"Zerin!" shouts Lach.

The sword finally releases from the wound and Zerin falls to the ground. The angry cat turns toward Zerin. The Fikron takes a step toward Zerin, the damage shows as its movement is severely limited.

Lach looks around for his sword, finally spotting it, he runs for it.

The cat growls at Zerin, but does not attack. Zerin sees the weakness and attacks. He swings his sword side to side catching the crippled cat several times, ripping into its flesh. Blood drips from the wounds, but only appears as sweat from the jet black fur that has helped in the sabotage of countless unsuspecting victims while they rested by a campfire or slept under the stars.

"You are finished," says Zerin.

Zerin steps to the Fikron and dodges a slow, weak swipe from the massive paws. Zerin stabs the Fikron in the chest, just missing the heart. The torturer now becomes the tortured. Zerin stabs again and the cat falls to its back struggling for breath as the blood from its wounds begins to fill its lungs. Zerin, with visions of the cat's torture of the dying Legna, jumps on top of the Fikron and stabs away, until the Fikron breathes no more.

Lach, with sword in hand, halts in his race to help his friend and stares in wonder at Zerin's great victory over this legendary creature.

"You have killed a Fikron," says Lach with a bit of admiration mixed with a little envy.

Zerin looks at Lach then looks toward where Gyran lay. He rushes to the Legna's side.

The Legna lays lifeless, apparently passing on sometime while the boys battled the Fikron. Zerin looks at him with sadness in his eyes and sighs. Lach walks up to his side.

"We have to bury him and his friend. They are brave warriors and deserve a warrior's burial," says Zerin.

Lach agrees, but then Zerin gets up and walks back over to the Fikron. Lach follows.

"What are you going to do with your trophy?" asks Lach.

Zerin says nothing, but pulls a bowl from his pack and

sets it to the side. Zerin cuts into the Fikron's chest and digs around as Lach looks on curiously.

"I talked with a wise old man and he spoke about the special power one is supposed to get if they ever kill a Fikron," Zerin says as he grabs something inside the chest cavity of the dead beast.

"What?" asks Lach, his tone unusually passive.

Zerin pulls and tugs at something inside the corpse then pulls his hand out of the chest and in it he holds the heart of the Fikron.

"I must drink of the blood of the Fikron," he says as he holds the large, mangled heart in the air, then lowers it over the bowl and squeezes. The dark red blood runs out into the bowl.

Lach stares on in disbelief as Zerin finishes squeezing the heart and takes the bowl in his hand and drinks.

"Are you sure?" asks Lach, staring strangely at his friend.

Zerin finishes his drink and wipes his mouth clean, then looks at Lach. The serious frown on his face is broken by a smile and laughter as he can't contain himself after seeing Lach's shocked expression.

"Suddenly my boisterous friend has fallen silent," says Zerin.

Lach stays silent, but smiles.

Zerin wipes his hands on some leaves nearby and walks over to the body of the Legna.

"We should hurry and bury these two before dark so that we can find a safe place to sleep," Zerin says as he looks for a good spot for a grave.

Lach joins him. They perform a quick ceremony then

set out again and journey on until dark then set up camp and go to sleep.

The land seems safer as Lach and Zerin begin to get further away from the dangerous areas around the Pryon mountains. Zerin walks proud of his feat, but Lach is more consumed with it.

"I do not like that I left that Fikron King to live and do as he pleases. I am considering turning back and taking my revenge, as I believe destiny has commanded," Lach says.

"We need to meet up with our friends. I am sure they are as worried about us as we are about them," says Zerin.

"You should have let me kill that Fikron. I could have taken him," says Lach.

"Your sword was lost and you were in danger. I was not going to stand by and hope for the best and risk seeing you meet the same fate as Gyran," says Zerin.

"Well now I must kill a Fikron, so that I can drink of its blood," Lach says, cringing at the thought.

"You will get your chance," says Zerin, sensing the envy tearing at Lach.

"It's just…," Lach pauses and grits his teeth.

Zerin notices the expression and asks, "Why does everything between us have to be a competition for you? Do you have to be better than me at everything?"

The desire to be the best usually consumed Lach and knowing that his rival had one up on him made it just that much worse, but he stays silent. Lach knows his biggest weakness is a lack of patience and he isn't going to give anyone the satisfaction of knowing how bad it burns him to not equal Zerin's feat. Of course Zerin already knows. He and Lach always had a strong connection.

"We are young, my dear Lach. I'm sure this will not be the last time that we explore these strange lands. You are a great warrior, and to conquer a Fikron will merely be one of the many great accomplishments you will achieve in your lifetime," Zerin says, knowing how to cool the temper of his longtime friend.

The whole day is nice. The sun shines with limited patches of white clouds dotting the light blue sky. The weather is warm and comfortable and shows in the boys more carefree demeanor. Seemingly out of the dangerous lands of the north, the boys begin to act like boys again.

"I wonder if we will run into the others before we get back home?" wonders Zerin.

"Normally I would say we will cover much more ground than they will, but they are probably eager to get home. They will probably beat us back, unless Juntor gets himself into trouble again," says Lach.

Both boys laugh.

"I wonder if they found Aragopia?" asks Lach.

"Gyran was not human, though he had a similar appearance than us. I definitely believe he was a Legna," says Zerin.

"Does that mean they met him in Aragopia, or did they just find where Legnas live?" asks Lach.

"I do not know, but no matter what happened, I am sure they will swear they found it," says Zerin.

"They will have to present a lot of evidence or some good stories before they convince me that they found that place," says Lach.

"I do not know, but I know there is a reason that so few people know about Aragopia and there is a reason we have never heard of anyone finding it," says Zerin.

"I am hoping that one day I can journey this way again and see for myself if such a place exists. Will you take that journey with me one day?" asks Lach

"Sure," answers Zerin.

Lach stops, triggering Zerin to do so as well.

"Make this promise my Arizz brother. Promise me that we will make this journey to discover Aragopia one day and to not return, until we are successful," demands a serious Lach.

Seeing the seriousness in Lach's face, Zerin nods and the boys bump forearms, nod at each other and continue.

"You know we will probably have to conquer the Trett before we get the chance to revive this journey. I have overheard my father complaining about the king lowering the age of the academy students that could be called up to fight," says Zerin.

"The sooner the better, I am ready to fight as soon as we get home. Something needs to be done. That weak king of ours is close to losing this war. When I get in, changes will happen, whether the superiors like it or not," says Lach.

"So you are going to take over the military, just like that. A boy, taking power from grown men in high places?" asks Zerin.

"The power is in the masses, not the few in power. If I can get the warriors on my side, they will choose who they follow," says Lach.

"How do you plan on doing that?" asks Zerin.

"Who would you follow, the conquering hero on a

distant battlefield or some weak man hiding on a throne many miles away?" asks Lach.

Zerin gets the point, but says, "I still keep a little bit of faith in the possibility of peace."

Lach doesn't answer for a moment then says. "You sound like your father again. I thought maybe some time away would get that crazy talk out of your head. Your father does not consider that some men are so evil, that the only way to deal with them is to kill them. The General is that kind of man."

"I am not like my father and I understand a man like The General needs to be killed, because there is no way he will ever accept anything less than total control. What I am saying is that if The General is done away with, we can establish peace with the Trett people and the Trett warriors," says Zerin.

Lach grunts and says. "Anyone loyal to that tyrant deserves death or at least, imprisonment."

"Most are not loyal to The General, but loyal to their family and friends who are Trett as well. I do not believe that all people under a certain leadership, especially under a tyrant, are as bad as that tyrant," says Zerin.

"If they do not agree, then they should stand against him. If they do not stand against him, then they are either traitors to the Arizz or spineless cowards who do not deserve the freedom we have in the first place," says Lach.

"A lot of people have more responsibilities than we do, being only responsible for ourselves. They have family to consider. They have to consider safety and they have to provide for their families," says Zerin.

"Cowards, I call them," says Lach.

"I say the problems are with the leaders. Let us be Arizz and let the Trett be Trett. Kill The General and any like him and then live and let live," says Zerin.

"Vengeance is another factor you haven't considered in your peace talk," says Lach. "How many Trett have killed our people? Are we to just forget?" he asks.

Zerin does not answer.

"No, we do not forget. We honor our dead by avenging their deaths," says Lach.

"Then where does it end?" Zerin asks himself as the boys continue on, silent now, as so many of their past debates have ended.

Night arrives not too long after the intense debate. The boys, now past the discussion talk about less adult subjects. They set up camp under a large tree, taking fewer precautions now that they are a comfortable distance from the strange north lands.

Chapter 15

Brenka-uku points toward a large bush that shutters even though there is no wind. Senokre and Juntor stare with swords drawn.

"Be ready," says Senokre, preparing for battle.

The bush rustles some more and then a large black cat walks out from behind, and with its fangs fully exposed, the Fikron snarls at the boys.

"It is only one. If it attacks, circle around it," commands Senokre.

The boys spread out and wait for the beast's assault.

"You are in foreign lands evil creature and you are outnumbered. Leave now and we will allow you to live," says Senokre.

The Fikron crouches and slowly approaches the boys, as if trying to get in range to lunge at whichever boys winds up closest.

"Attack the legs first and attempt to cripple it then attack the head or the heart," Senokre orders.

The stare down continues for a few intense moments, then growling from behind the boys sends shivers down their spines. They turn to see that two more Fikrons have joined the standoff.

"Circle up, back to back. Stand strong and show no fear," says Senokre.

The boys stand surrounded by the three Fikrons as thoughts of life and death go through their minds. They keep hope that they can still defeat these creatures. Their numbers are even.

The snarling cats watch the boys, but do not attack. As if they are observing their prey, searching for a weakness to exploit, they wait. Of course, they could be waiting for something else.

"A snapping of a twig draws attention to the entrance of yet another Fikron, followed by two more. The first three Fikrons look to the new group of Fikrons.

"It is starting to look like we are going to take a little longer to get home than we planned," Juntor says as he squints, looking past the Fikrons, toward the distant horizon.

The second group walks close to the boys, observing and studying them, walking around them and occasionally sniffing at them.

A Fikron stops and speaks. "You are young like the one called Lach, but you are not him."

It is the Fikron King.

The boys stare, shocked that the creature can speak.

"Do you know this boy I speak of?" asks the Fikron King.

"I know him," answers Senokre, defiantly.

"But he is not here?" asks the Fikron King.

"No," answers Juntor.

"Do you know where he is?" asks the Fikron King.

"We have not seen him for many days now. Have you?" asks Juntor with a smirk.

The Fikron looks upon Juntor, interested in his boldness.

"It is too bad, for now I no longer need you," says the Fikron King. "We shall see how bold you are after you watch your own blood flow from your mangled bodies."

Juntor smiles while Brenka-uku and Senokre stare at him, unsure of his reasoning.

"Perhaps it is you who will see his own blood," says Juntor.

The Fikron King looks at the bold little boy, amazed at his arrogance and smirks. "Do not confuse bravery with stupidity, child," it says.

"I said when I came on this adventure that I would create a song to tell of this adventure, and not until right now, have I come up with some of the words to that song," says Juntor.

The Fikron King still stares at the boy in amazement, putting off his planned attack for the moment, mesmerized by this creature he has had such little contact with, other than the few screams they make just before he finishes them off.

Time seems to stop and all things seem to be focusing on the unfolding event. Birds circle overhead as if trying to find the best vantage point to see the impending battle. The clouds in the sky seem to have stopped their travel through the air, like they too want to observe the showdown below.

There is silence as both groups seem to be tuning up their increasing senses, their bodies adapting to war mode. They stand waiting for the other's move. Sweat glistens on the boys' faces as the sun bears down. The air is hot and dry and the black cats pant with their tongues hanging out of their mouths. All things signify an approaching bloodbath, but whose blood, will only be known in a few moments.

The silence and concentrations are broken as Juntor speaks, in a poetic tone. "As the rumble from the ground begins to shake our feet, the approach of hooves driven in fleet…"

A rumbling sound carries itself over the hills in the distance.

"…no longer a sound but a coming storm…"

The rumbling builds and shakes all of the participants' feet. The Fikron's begin to shake. One of the Fikrons growls in Fikron language, "He has put a curse on the land."

"…to a threat that is no more," Juntor finishes.

Suddenly a legion of horsemen attack directly into the Fikron mass. The black beasts scatter in fear as the boys duck for cover. Dust fills the air and to see what is happening becomes difficult. The sounds of swords and grunts and horses and screeches fill the air.

Juntor tries to make out all that is happening through the dry cloud of dust. He sees many men on horses fighting with the dangerous cats. One man in particular catches Juntor's eye through the brown cloud and he observes this brave warrior. A green sheath is on his arm.

"Ranishi," says Juntor with a smile.

Juntor stands star struck for a moment, and before he can come out of his daze and in mere moments the rumble begins to fade and the air begins to clear. In the distance, the surviving Fikrons run for their lives and the horsemen give chase.

Now all that is left are the boys. Senokre and Brenka-uku stand and they wipe the dust off their clothes.

Brenka-uku points toward a set of trees on top of a small hill and says, "I saw the one that talked, sneak away."

Amazed by Juntor's bravery, Senokre asks him, "How did you know?"

"I saw a small cloud of dust in the distance. After I watched for a moment, I saw horsemen riding this way," answers Juntor. "I believe one to be Ranishi. He had the green sheath."

"You saw Ranishi?" asks an amazed Senokre.

Juntor smiles and nods his head.

An approaching noise draws the boys out of their moment and they face the oncoming threat with swords drawn. Their fiery expressions change as they see the source of the incoming racket. It is Lach and Zerin racing to the noise they had heard.

Smiles and greetings take the moment as the boys welcome the reunion. They share stories as quickly as possible. With so much to tell and everybody talking, only bits and pieces resonate. They will surely have to retell their stories more thoroughly later. Right now, they are just happy to see each other.

They sit for a few moments and continue to talk and just enjoy each other's company, but the moment is lost when

Brenka-uku repeats something he said earlier that was missed.

"I believe I saw the one that talks avoid the horsemen and sneak away over that hill over there," Brenka-uku says.

"Talks," asks Lach, "a Fikron that talks? There was a Fikron here that could talk in our language?"

"But we are far from Aragopia," says Senokre.

Lach stands and looks toward the hill.

Zerin looks at Lach and knows, but tries to deter his friend's intentions and says, "We should start working our way home. We are so close now."

Lach does not respond to Zerin, but says, "I will be right back."

Lach walks away from the boys.

"Where is he going?" asks Senokre.

"He is going to fulfill his mission," answers Zerin.

"Should we go with him?" asks Senokre.

"We will, but let us give him a moment and then we will go check on him," says Zerin.

"He is going to kill the Fikron, isn't he?" asks Juntor admiringly.

Zerin nods his head, not telling his impressed pals that he himself has already slain a Fikron.

As Lach reaches the top of the hill, he gazes across the horizon. There just fifty yards away is the Fikron King walking away.

Apparently the Fikron King hid amongst a group of bushes during the raid by the horsemen. It waited there until the noises from the battle disappeared, and waited a little longer until it felt it was safe to get back to familiar lands and the safety of the canyon.

Lach begins to rush in a fast walk toward the giant

black cat. The Fikron's pace is slow and it is unaware of the approaching threat. Finally it hears oncoming footsteps on the hardened ground.

The Fikron stops and turns. Lach stops. The two stare at each other, trying to anticipate the other's next move.

"Why do you hide, while your friends die by the swords of your enemies?" asks Lach.

The Fikron stands silent, glaring at Lach.

Lach looks over the Fikron, searching for any characteristic that would separate this Fikron from the rest. He needs to see if the Fikron can speak.

Lach taunts the black menace. "A coward I see standing in front of me. So powerful and brave when he is protected by his minions, now I see the true grit of the legendary Fikron King."

The Fikron continues to glare at Lach, showing neither an intention of retreating nor a desire to attack.

"Just a cat, a larger version of the pets we keep in our homes or the strays we throw our scraps to, nothing more," says Lach.

The Fikron takes a moment to glance around at their surroundings, searching for any threat other than the boy in front of him then turns back to stare at his challenger.

"It does not matter if you are he or are not the one I seek. I am going to kill you regardless. So do not pretend you do not understand me, or that you cannot respond. Either way, your head shall be a present to my mentor when I return home," Lach says as he raises his sword to ready for a fight.

"Mouthy little boy," responds the Fikron King, "Do you think I fear you any less here than I did when I chained you to my wall as my own pet?"

"You told me that you did not kill me, because you believed I was of the line of Gokar, killers of many Fikrons. So you kept me alive, because you wanted to see a descendant of Gokar as your prisoner," says Lach.

"The family of Gokar has killed many of my kind, yes, but I have personally killed many, many of that line. So to kill you would be no real achievement and as before, by the end of this day, you will be on a chain once again."

Of course, as you can see, they could never kill me. I have proven too mighty, even for a family with such a legacy. No descendant of Gokar will ever kill me," proclaims the Fikron King.

Lach smiles and says, "Most that have been around as long as you are wise, yet you make amateur mistakes. You should have killed me when your minions ambushed and captured me, for now you have kept alive the one that will be your slayer. Of course your biggest mistake is that of assumption. I treasure the Medallion of Gokar, yes, but I am not of his line. I am an orphan and I do not know my line."

The Fikron King is surprised by the revelation and says, "This is disappointing news. Now to kill you will be no great feat, but just another notch in my glorious mission to destroy all humans. An orphan no less, an unwanted child of an unknown family line that no one knew when they were alive and no one remembers after their death. When your kind tells the histories of this land, they will make no mention of the orphan I exterminated on this day. Prepare to die young one."

Lach refutes, "Wrong again mighty creature, for those who tell the histories of this land will say, 'An orphan', an unwanted child as you say, 'ended the reign of the king of the

Fikrons, Alohessy's most evil creation'."

Lach attacks. The Fikron, caught off guard, desperately defends against the onslaught of swings and stabs of the youth's sword. It finally jumps clear and sets in an attack ready crouch. Lach resets himself then attacks again.

Zerin and the other boys reach the top of the hill and look toward the battle. Senokre pulls out his sword and takes a step toward the skirmish. Zerin grabs his shoulder and holds him back.

"Wait, Senokre. Only if Lach is in danger will we enter the fight," he says.

Another assault by Lach is dodged by the black cat and it swipes at Lach's legs, barely catching his ankle. Lach's momentum sends him stumbling to the ground. The cat pounces. But Lach rolls out of the way, catching the tip of his sword against the Fikron's front leg, opening a small wound. Lach stands. The Fikron licks its wound, undeterred it lunges for Lach as Lach lunges for it.

Senokre stands, anxiously watching the battle. His head and body move, like he is in the battle himself, ducking and dodging like a boxing fan watching his favorite fighter.

The other boys anxiously watch as well, but not as animated. Zerin stands quietly, his anxiety showing only in his eyes. He believes Lach can win this battle, but it would only take one strike of the Fikrons massive claws ripping into Lach's flesh, to leave his friend mortally wounded. But he also knows that Lach would not accept passing up this opportunity, no matter what. The death of his friend may hold no match to the wrath that he would face from Lach if he took away a sole victory over this creature of legendary myths.

A lunging strike by the Fikron catches Lach and knocks him several feet, sliding across the rough turf. Lach lies still, not moving. The Fikron cautiously approaches, with its stance low, waiting for a sneaky attack by the boy. The Fikron circles Lach as he arrives to the fallen body. There is no movement. The Fikron stays cautious, watching Lach's sword the whole while he sniffs at the unmoving young warrior.

"I will not fall for your tricks, and do not pretend that I need more than a small rake of my claws across your throat to end this battle and your unknown line," says the King.

Lach moans, like someone coming out of unconsciousness. The Fikron looks at him, believing now that Lach is not faking. The momentary, minimal surprise is just enough and Lach swings his sword with all his might. The razor-sharp blade slashes into the meat of the Fikron's front leg. The sword goes clean through, bone and all, sending the Fikron tumbling away with its severed leg staying put and falling beside Lach.

Lach gets up slowly. He stands, like a great warrior rising from near defeat, preparing for the final blow to conquer his enemy. Blood pours, from a large gash on his forehead, down his face. Now he has an appearance more threatening than even that of a Fikron in its most ferocious moments. Lach is the king of this battlefield.

The Fikron King stumbles to keep its distance. Blood pours out of the stump that used to be a leg. The evil in its eyes has changed and for the first time in its life, it shows the fear that so many of its victims have just before taking their last breath.

"You are finished. Show some honor for the end of

your dishonorable life and bow to accept the final blow," says Lach, slowly inching toward the Fikron.

The damaged beast looks around for a place to run. It still has three legs and may still be able to outrun this menace it has encountered.

"There is no real bravery in evil, only opportunity," says Lach. "Do not run, your death is certain."

The Fikron makes a run for it. It is correct in that it could outrun Lach, because Lach limps after it, exposing an injured foot.

"Coward," Lach yells as he stops and watches.

The Fikron King believes that it has escaped after looking back and seeing no pursuit. But when it looks back toward the direction of its flight, the crippled cat is met with a roadblock. Zerin and the boys stand with swords drawn, stopping the great beast's exit. The Fikron backs away as the boys close in on it. A few paces backwards and the Fikron decides to run in the opposite direction. The move is fatal. The king turns right into the tip of Lach's sword and Lach finishes the final blow, pushing the sharp steel into the Fikron's chest. The Fikron's eyes tell the tale. Fear, surprise and disbelief all show as centuries of dominance all end at the tip of an orphan's blade. The Fikron falls to the ground and its breathing gets more and more shallow, until the threat becomes a corpse.

Lach takes a deep breath and exhales, looks at his friends and nods his head. Excitement begins to take Senokre, Juntor and Brenka-uku and they jump around and stare at the felled beast of legend.

Zerin walks to Lach and stands at his side. "Well done. You will be in the stories of legends now. But right now you know what has to be done," he says.

Lach nods his head, and to the shock of the other three he begins to cut into the dead Fikron King's chest. Zerin assists him. They go through the process and Lach pulls out the heart, squeezes the blood into Zerin's bowl and drinks the blood of Fikron King.

The boys' expressions never change. They cannot believe what Lach is doing and are grossed out.

Zerin looks at them and smiles. "We'll explain it to you on the way home."

While Lach cleans up his hands and face. Zerin and Senokre sever the head from the dark beast and strap it to Zerin's back.

"We will take turns carrying this for you, Lach, since you are injured. This will be proof of our journey."

"Thank you Zerin, but I wish only to show the head to Olkar so that he may know that vengeance has come to the creature that took his father."

Lach rubs the Medallion of Gokar which hangs around his neck and pride fills his being.

The boys set fire to the carcass of the Fikron King and set out on the final leg of their journey home.

Chapter 16

The smoke of the burning carcass can be seen for miles as the boys walk across the prairie. Despite Lach's injury, their pace is good and as night begins to fall they arrive to the top of one of the hills in the meadow that make up Arizz lands.

"Look," yells Juntor, "the Great City!"

In the haze of the evening horizon, great walls surrounding many small twinkling lights show in the distance. The city is still several miles away, but the site of their home gives the boys comfort and they set camp right on that spot. While many of their recent nights have been comforted by the twinkling of the stars in the sky, tonight's comfort will come by the twinkling of the lights of the Great City, standing as an oasis in a desert of isolation. Tomorrow they will be home.

Morning feels like the best morning of their lives.
Happy and excited, the boys pack up their things. Energized
by the site of their home the boys spend the last few hours of
their journey joking and laughing and arrive upon the city
around mid-morning. The vendors are out, selling various
items to residence of the city and to visitors traveling from the
outer Arizz zones. The boys walk unnoticed through the
hustle and bustle and through the towering gates of the large
city.

Inside is the same as outside, people buying and
selling, carts going to and fro. The shouts of academy
students can be heard in the distance as they practice in the
training yard. Lach longs to begin training again so he can
join the war as soon as possible.

As he looks toward the academy, he recognizes a
familiar face and tells the others. "Uh oh, our first trouble,
here comes Juntor's father."

Juntor sees his father approaching and his body tenses.
Even though he tries to keep it a secret, his friends are aware
of his problems at home.

Juntor's father's name is Raymuth. He was once a
decorated trainer of many Arizz warriors. But a head injury
after an accident on a horse left him with some brain damage
and he was unable to continue his successful career. Later his
wife left him for an outlander and she fell at the hands of that
same man. Raymuth began drinking and his life has been that
of shame and sorrow ever since.

Juntor hated his father and wished for his death. He
was terribly ashamed of his family and wished he was an

orphan, so that no one would know of whose bloodline he had descended.

Raymuth approaches enraged and somewhat intoxicated. He grabs Juntor's arm and with his free hand slaps his son across the face twice, right in front of everybody. Juntor's humiliation outweighs the pain of the blows.

As Raymuth raises his hand for another blow, a defiant hand catches his arm and stops the strike in its path. It is Lach's hand and with his other hand he pulls his sword and places it at the throat of Raymuth.

"Release him," Lach says with a snarl. "I have fought evil beyond your imagination on this journey and will not blink at the thought of sending you to join them in the depths."

Raymuth releases Juntor and backs off. He eyes Lach for a moment then steps to Juntor and smacks him again.

"You better tell your friends to never touch me or threaten me again. You are in more trouble now than ever," says Raymuth.

Raymuth grabs Juntor and leads him away from the others. Lach runs up behind Raymuth and kicks him in the back of the knee, knocking the abusive man to his knees then he hits Raymuth in the face, knocking him to the ground. Lach stands over the fallen man. Raymuth looks up at Lach to see only a fist, striking him in the face over and over.

Juntor watches the assault, unsure of what to do.

"Stop Lach, you are hurting him," says Juntor.

Lach pauses, still standing over the battered man. "How many times has he hurt you? How many more times is he going to hurt you? He needs to learn how it feels."

"You can stay with me and my family, Juntor," says Zerin. "You don't have to go through this anymore."

Juntor looks at Zerin. A thump from another Lach punch to Raymuth's face draws Juntor's attention back to his father. Raymuth no longer has the look of a violent abusive father. He now looks upon his son, as if begging for mercy and unsure of why he is receiving this beating.

Juntor remembers words that he shared with Quynn. "Stop, Lach," he says as he blocks Lach's next blow.

Lach backs away confused. Juntor bends down beside Raymuth and helps him up. Raymuth place his arm around Juntor, needing support after the dizzying shots.

"I understand now and it is OK, Lach. Thank you for protecting me, but I realize now that my father is sick and he needs me, more than I need him. I will not abandon him. If I do not care for him, then who will? He will not abuse me any longer. I understand that he needs help and I am the only one who will. He is my father, no matter what, and starting today things will be different."

Raymuth leans on Juntor with tears in his eyes. He kisses his son's head and they turn and Juntor helps his father back to their home.

The boys watch Juntor and Raymuth disappear in the crowd of people in the courtyard.

"Why would he want to live with that trash?" asks Lach

"Because sometimes, love is better than violence, Lach," says Zerin.

Lach frowns at the thought and says, "What love does that man deserve?"

"Maybe it's not what he deserves, but what he needs,"

says Zerin.

Sensing a long debate, Senokre interrupts Lach and Zerin and says, "Brenka is going to stay with my family while he is here. Of course I need to ask, but you know my family. They love visitors, so we'll see you guys tomorrow. We can share stories about how much trouble we are in."

Lach and Zerin smile as Senokre and Brenka-uku walk away.

"Well, we did it. We went on a great quest, that few have ever tried and we came back alive. Now I must go and face my father. I will be OK. I do not need you to rough up Salazaar," Zerin says with a smile. "He might try to defend himself and ruin his stand on peace at all costs."

Lach smiles and the boys bump forearms.

"I am excited to present Olkar with his family medallion and of course the head," says Lach.

"Oh yeah," says Zerin.

Zerin had forgotten about the head, now covered with some rags, on his back. He hands it over to Lach and the two boys stare at each other. For as much rivalry that exists between the boys, just as much admiration exists as well.

Lach smiles, turns toward his home and as he walks away, says, "See you tomorrow."

Zerin watches his friend walk away and says, "See you tomorrow."

Characters

Alohessy- The first being (Zirca lord) created by Kron. Obsessed with power, he became the evil that haunts Thrae.

Arak- A Fikron that lives in Aragopia and no longer desires to do evil.

Brenka-uku- A Chimihog who sought adventure, was imprisoned by Wilber, and freed by the boys and joined them on their journey.

Brigal- The third being (Zirca lord) created by Kron. Fearful of Alohessy, he joins his evil brother in the battles with Chryson. Creates Aragopia in order to hide from Alohessy and repent of his ways.

Brilka-tuku- The Chimihog that is Brenka-uku's father. Lives in Nork's compound.

Chryson- The second being (Zirca lord) created by Kron. Killed by Alohessy and Brigal with Alohessy's sword.

Doran- The first human created by Kron, given to Dorisha as her own child.

Dorisha- The fourth being (Zirca lord) created by Kron. She is eventually killed by Alohessy after being forced to produce five offspring (Zircas) for him. Mother of the first human, Doran.

Fikron King- The leader of Alohessy's most evil creations. The only creature that can speak outside of Aragopia.

Finon – Zerin's mentor at the youth military academy.

the General- Bloodthirsty leader of the Trett.

Gokar- Great warrior of the past. An ancestor of Olkar.

Gorka-tuku- Brenka-uku's mother

Gyran- A Legna that lives in Aragopia, sent to search for Lach and Zerin.

Hedgeparth- Old man that tells the boys of the mythical land called Aragopia.

Hermak- A giraffe that the boys meet when in Aragopia.

Honkra-ruku- Leader of the Chimihogs

Hrun- A high ranking member of the fat tribe that tried to eat Juntor.

Iras- Giraffe and guide in Aragopia.

Jeroquy- One of two brothers responsible for defeating the Zirca revolt, also responsible for the split between the Arizz and Trett.

Jirick- Old lady who greets Zerin in Vaugne.

Juntor- Youngest member of the journey, he deals with self esteem issues and home issues.

Kron- The creator of the planet of Thrae. Tricked by Alohessy, it is said that he is lost underneath the Pryon Mountains still searching for Dorisha.

Lach- A very aggressive member of the journey, he seeks challenge. He is a very talented youth warrior who often clashes with Zerin over ideas.

Mareege- Old man in the village of Vaugne who talks with Zerin.

Nork- The mysterious man who lives amongst the chimihogs. A very paranoid personality.

Norka-ruku- The wife of Honkra-ruku.

Nostradan- A Legna who greets the boys when they first enter Aragopia.

Olkar- Aging hero warrior of the Arizz. He is the mentor of Lach.

Plythagor- One of two brothers responsible for defeating the Zirca revolt, also responsible for the split between the Arizz and Trett.

Quynn- Oldest boy on the journey, he is viewed as a future great leader of the Arizz military.

Ranishi- The human who killed Alohessy and won the war that put humans in power. Uncertain of his whereabouts, many say he lives in Aragopia where one can live forever.

Raymuth- Alcoholic father of Juntor and one of the main causes of Juntor's lack of confidence.

Salazaar- Father of Zerin, he is a powerful politician who opposes war and often quarrels with Zerin.

Sarah- Motherly figure that the boys meet in Aragopia.

Senokre- Instigator of the search for Aragopia, he is the most normal of the boys and just seeks adventure.

Sren- The father of Wren, of the fat tribe that tried to eat Juntor.

Surl- A Legna who leads the boys back to their common lands.

Tiriach- Evil orphan who taught the Zircas their powers and attempted to take over Thrae.

Wilber- Bizarre little man that lives in the darkness of the Caves of Talpri. Kidnapped Brenka-uku.

Wren- Son of Sren, who is killed by Lach.

Yatique- Little boy in the village of Vaugne that first meets Zerin.

Zerin- Conflicted over beliefs, he seeks the right answer in all situations. A very talented youth warrior, he often clashes with Lach of ideas.

Creatures and Beings of Thrae

Albinogators- Remnants of Alohessy's wars with humans, these white Alligators now live in the many rivers of Thrae.

Chimihogs- Small and stout fuzzy creatures with pig-like faces, they live with Nork in his compound.

Fikrons- The most evil creation of Alohessy used in the wars with humans, they now stay clear of highly populated areas, but if ever a few humans drift into their territories they will attack. Not aware of Alohessy's death, they are still set out on their mission to battle Kron. (Fight Kron)

Giraffes- One of the many beautiful and good creatures created by Kron in the beginning. They are rare in highly populated human areas and are a joy to see by travelers.

Humans- Kron's answer to the Zirca-lords, having no special magic powers, but a special characteristic, souls.

Legnas- Beings created by Kron for the wars with Alohessy. Due to Kron's fears, their powers were limited and they were ultimately defeated. The remaining are said to live in Aragopia.

Zircas- Descendants of the five offspring of Alohessy and Dorisha. They are capable of having great powers, but must learn them first. Plythagor and Jeroquy conquered the Zirca uprising and enslaved any remaining Zircas.

Zirca-lords- The first four creations of Kron with many powers. They became a menace to Thrae and battled till all, but one, were killed. Only Dorisha had favor with Kron and that is why it is said he still searches for her in the Caves of Talpri, believing she is still alive.

Tribes, lands and landmarks

Arizz- The largest and original tribe of humans. The Arizz control the Great City though they often battle with the Trett.

Caves of Talpri- A labyrinth of mines below the Pryon Mountains. Even Kron can become lost in the maze and is said to still be there.

Fountains of Talpri- Many fountains spread over many acres. It is said the waters in them contain magic powers, but only a few know what kind.

The Great City- The largest city in Thrae, whoever holds control of it, rule over Thrae.

Miklidor- A once thriving land, it is now poisoned and many strange creatures roam the desolate territory.

Outlands- Far to the west, there lay many small tribes of people who want to live their own ways, different from common ways. They live in these unclaimed lands.

Pryon Mountains- The largest mountain range in all of Thrae. The mountain range can be seen from all locations known to man.

Suna-Noru- The lands of a former religious tribe, now mostly abandoned. Old temples set all over the land.

Trett- A tribe that used to be part of the Arizz, they now seek to control Thrae. They are led by the General.

Vaugne- A small village hidden on the edge of the Pryon mountains. Separated from the rest of the tribes during the wars with Alohessy, it holds many secrets of the past.

Don't miss the Journey to the Horse Realm!

Follow Lach and Zerin and friends on their next adventure as they go in search of the legendary Horse Realm. Excitement and chaos follow as they encounter old friends, new tribes and bizarre strangers. New tests and new learning experiences wait as they are forced to make grown-up decisions as friendships are tested and trust is blurred. Don't miss:

The Battles of Thrae:
Journey to the Horse Realm

coming

April 2012

visit

www.TheBattlesofThrae.com

Excerpt from Journey to the Horse Realm

Under the green foliage, the downpour is minimized with only a few drops penetrating the leaf canopy. The boys take off their backpacks and toss them on the ground.

The trees are large and the boys do not see that they have company, also taking refuge under the trees from the rain. Grunting noises come from the other side of one of the trees. Zerin peeks around to see an old man, apparently waking from a nap. Zerin recognizes the old man. It is Hedgeparth.

"Hedgeparth, I was worried we had missed you before we set out, but here you are," says Senokre.

"Young adventurers, I am glad I have this time to see you before you leave. I must tell a little about my journey before you go, if you will give an old man a few moments?" asks Hedgeparth.

The boys agree and they all sit around Hedgeparth. With the rain beating against the covering of the patch of trees and the occasional thunder rumbling in the distance, the mood is set for a good story.

Hedgeparth tells of his journey near Miklidor again and his last minute decision to back out of his plan to journey into the poisoned land. He speaks of seeing an army of men that appeared to him to be of some kind of royalty. He speaks of almost drowning as he crossed a river and getting his bad foot caught in a hole under the water. He speaks of taking refuge in a tree for two nights after he sensed the presence of a Fikron, a fear never proven. He speaks of seeing a Giraffe, which the boys had told him about after they had returned from their adventure. He covers bits and pieces about things he saw for the first time and then finally he arrives at the part of the story which he is most excited to tell the boys about.

"I came across another old traveler like myself. We spoke for a few moments, of things we had seen and heard. Then, he asked me had I heard of a particular place, a majestic place where most humans have never ventured."

Hedgeparth pauses and gives the boys a stern look and continues. "At first I thought he was going to speak of Aragopia, but I did not say a word. After what you had told me, I feel it is better that as few people as possible should know about the mythical lands beyond the Pryon Mountains.

So I let him continue his story and to my surprise, he was not speaking of Aragopia. This land he spoke of has managed to avoid contamination by the poisons that pollute Miklidor, yet is close enough to the tainted country that very few men know of its existence. This land has one special characteristic that sets it apart from the land we roam."

Hedgeparth pauses again to allow the boys interest to grow and enjoys as they sit in anxious silence for him to reveal the secret of this new land. Hedgeparth smiles and continues.

"This great territory is called the Horse Realm. There roam hundreds and hundreds of the most beautiful and splendid breeds of horses ever seen. It is said if a man is true enough, brave enough and deserving enough that if he travels to the Horse Realm, he will find the perfect horse which will bond with him and be his loyal steed till death."

The boys' eyes light up, especially Lach's.

"Why did you not go and find your horse?" asks Lach.

"I am an old man, far too old to wander a strange land looking for one horse. Besides, I prefer to walk," answers Hedgeparth.

Lach looks at Zerin and says, "We must find this Horse Realm. I must find the horse that waits for me."

"Do not allow yourself to believe this will be an easy exercise. Not all of the horses there are accepting of humans. As I understand it, if a horse does not bond with its destined human and the human passes on, the horse develops a deep frustration. It is as if it is missing a part of its soul and it becomes lost in its mind and let's just say, not so friendly," finishes Hedgeparth.

Not seeming to hear Hedgeparth's warning Lach looks at his friends and says, "We should take a detour on our way to take Brenka home. We should really find this Horse Realm."

"Maybe we should check with Brenka. He may want to hurry home. He has not seen his people in a very long time," says Zerin.

Lach looks to Brenka-uku with his ever demanding glare. Brenka-uku does not need the extra nudge by Lach. He loves adventure and was preparing to suggest a journey that direction anyway.

"I'm ready to see this Horse Realm," Brenka-uku says.

Zerin nods and says, "OK, that was easy enough. Then when this rain subsides, we share turn our journey west and find this land of horses."

The Battles of Thrae:
Journey to the Horse Realm

www.TheBattlesofThrae.com

Coming Soon

THE BATTLES OF THRAE TRILOGY

Part 1: A Bond Broken
Part 2: Promises of a Stranger
Part 3: In the Darkest Hour

When friends quarrel and vengeance takes hold on otherwise logical minds, the fate of mankind comes into play. Don't miss Lach and Zerin and friends as the battles between the Trett and Arizz go from distant battlefields to their very front doors.

As a war between rivals blinds them to even greater threats, no longer is the goal to control the land, but the goal is to prevent the extinction of mankind on Thrae.

Who will overcome and who will betray and what, if any, is the answer to ensure that mankind can continue?

THE BATTLES OF THRAE TRILOGY

www.TheBattlesofThrae.com

www.ingramcontent.com/pod-product-compliance
Lightning Source LLC
Chambersburg PA
CBHW050319200626
46808CB00023BA/1780